Large _____

D1626968

WF
Bo.
91 HR

| FEB 2 0 2001 | DATE DUE | |
|---|---|---|
| AUG 2 0 | | |
| MAY 2 4 2004 | | |
| JUN 0 1 2004  HA | | |
| FEB 2 6 2007 | | |
| | | |
| | | |
| | | |
| | | |
| | | |
| | | |

# MORGETTE ON THE
# BARBARY COAST

*Also by G.G. Boyer*
*in Thorndike Large Print*

THE GUNS OF MORGETTE
MORGETTE IN THE YUKON

# MORGETTE ON THE BARBARY COAST

## by G. G. Boyer

**Thorndike Press • Thorndike, Maine**

**Library of Congress Cataloging in Publication Data:**

Boyer, Glenn G.
  Morgette on the Barbary Coast.

  Reprint. Originally published: New York: Walker, 1985.
  1. Large type books.  I. Title.
[PS3552.O8926M63  1985]      813'.54      85-20972
ISBN 0-89621-674-8 (lg. print : alk. paper)

All the characters and events portrayed in this story are fictitious.

Large Print edition available through arrangement with
Walker and Company, New York.

Cover design by Mimi Harrison.

# MORGETTE ON THE BARBARY COAST

# Chapter 1

Forrest Twead had fled St. Michael, Alaska, on a steamer bound for San Francisco. That was the only thing Dolf Morgette was sure he knew as he came down the gangplank from the *Alaskan* and planted his boots firmly on the Embarcadero. He glanced around warily in the foggy darkness. Knowing Twead, he realized that from this moment forward his life could be in danger. Twead had, beyond a doubt, hired the killing of Dolf's friend, Harvey Parrent. And Twead knew Dolf — knew he'd be after him.

Now Dolf was on a cold trail, not knowing whether Twead would be here or had merely passed through. If he were in Frisco, he might still have connections who would hide him. They would quite probably also be the type who would do his dirty work for him — especially for a price. And Twead was well heeled, having, true to form, skipped out with someone else's bankroll from Alaska.

Frisco's night air was cloyingly chilly, causing Dolf to shiver. He felt very much alone, although he could hear the bantering voices of stevedores working somewhere up the wet wharf, where several dim lights flickered through the mist, reflecting in puddles. A distant bell buoy donged mournfully from somewhere over the dark water. It all recalled how very much alone he really was in the world. He dismally reflected that he'd lost his little Margaret and their year-old son, Henry, just a few months before, drowned when the ice had gone out of Sky Pilot River, flooding everything with almost no warning. It was a jarring reminder of just how transient life was, and the memory cast its inevitable heavy pall of gloom over him. If time healed, it was not working very fast in his case. The memory brought the usual lump to his throat and mistiness to his eyes. His grim mood was lifted by the arrival of Joe, the *Alaskan's* purser and Dolf's special sidekick on this trip, personally trundling his trunk down the gangplank as he'd promised. Joe had taken him in tow when he discovered he would be new to San Francisco.

"Gotta put up at the Palace," Joe had insisted, "even if it's only for one night. Ya never seen nothin' like it. One night won't break ya."

As a matter of fact, Dolf was moderately well off for the first time in his life as a result of good luck in the Sky Pilot gold strike. It was the only good thing that had happened to him there. Still, he didn't hate the country. His best friends were there, and he planned to return someday if his search for Twead was successful.

"I'll run your trunk over to the shed and you can call the Palace on the telephone and have 'em send over a hack," Joe was saying as they moved through the damp gloom. "I'll go back fer yer dog. The Palace'll have a place to keep him. They could probably put up an elephant if they had to. It's some place, like I said."

Dolf suspected that Joe was trying to see his face in the dark to see how the "telephone" remark had struck him. Coming from Alaska it could be possible he'd never seen a telephone, much less that he'd be apt to know how to use one. As it happened, some of the first telephones in the U.S. had been put in at Pinebluff up in Idaho, when the mines first boomed there. It was Dolf's home district. He'd also had one in the marshal's office at Ft. Belton, Montana.

"You know the Palace's number?" was all he said.

Joe grinned in the darkness, realizing the

9

city boys had lost round one.

"Ask Central," he said dryly. "I can't remember."

By the time Joe returned with Dolf's big hound, Jim Too, Dolf had phoned for a room and learned that the hotel had kennel facilities. But a hack wasn't to be had just then. The R. R. Ferry was due in, and the canny hack drivers had all converged at the ferry landing.

Jim Too seemed as happy to get on land as Dolf had been. He jumped all over Dolf and Joe. The big dog acted as though he hadn't seen him for weeks, even though Dolf had been down with him and his horse, Wowakan, for hours each day on board the *Alaskan*.

Dolf scratched Jim Too's head and back affectionately. When the frolic was over, he told Joe, "It'll be a while for a hack. The ferry is just getting in, they told me."

"I shudda remembered," Joe said. "Why not just walk down to the ferry building? It's only a coupla blocks. We're on Pacific, it's on Market. Let's see — that's four blocks down that way. Ya could see the lights if it wasn't so damn misty. Can't miss it, though. There'll be a slew of hacks and people millin' around. I'll send your trunk over to the Palace as soon as I can."

Dolf shook hands with Joe and gave him a gold fiver.

"Look me up before you ship out," Dolf invited. "We can have a beer or two, maybe dinner somewhere on me. I appreciate all you've done."

"Aw g'wan," Joe said. "I din' do much. I'll see you around."

A half block from where they left Joe, the city was another world. The fog had thickened, and but for the buildings to his right, Dolf would have been hard put to keep on course. A couple of sailors passed, curiously eyeing a big man and dog silently making their way here at night. There was a gaslight at each corner, but in midblock it was dark enough to make walking uncertain. Somewhere behind him Dolf could hear a horse-drawn vehicle approaching and wondered how whoever it was could see to stay on the street rather than drive off the wharf.

His first warning of peril was Jim Too's ominous growl. Dolf's first thought was of another dog. He knew better when Jim Too spun and lunged at someone who had slipped up behind him, fastening his huge jaws on a leg. Whoever it was cried out once in alarm and then raised his arm with some weapon in it to strike at the dog. Dolf's response was almost a reflex. He snaked his snub-nosed sheriff's model .45 from its shoulder rig and fired at the middle

11

of their assailant. As he did a second figure emerged from the darkness; Dolf covered him instantly, but he only looked once and fled. Meanwhile the first man had crumpled to the sidewalk, dropping his weapon to the pavement with a metallic clang. Dolf swept a glance all around to make sure there were no other potential attackers near, then picked up the weapon. He was surprised to find it was a long-handled hatchet.

A police whistle shrieked somewhere in the distance. He supposed the pistol shot had attracted the beat cop. He wondered if he should stick or try to disappear and avoid the inevitable, since he had no desire to see his arrival announced on the front page of every newspaper in the U.S. Before he could decide, the vehicle that had been moving up behind him pulled over.

"I saw them run by me," the driver announced. He leaped out of his rig and stooped over the fallen body. "Chinese hatchet man." He peered closely at Dolf. "You one of my boys?" Without waiting for an answer, he said, "I guess not."

The police whistle sounded again, and running feet could be heard somewhere in the near distance. "That cop must have got some reinforcements and got brave enough to come see," the newcomer said. Then, "Jump in, I'll get you to hell out of here fast. Yer dog'll follow, won't he?"

Dolf didn't hesitate. He didn't know who his benefactor was, but it was strictly a beggars-can't-be-choosers situation. His instinct told him this man was all right. The driver made a sweeping turn and drove rapidly the way he'd come, clucking the horses into a fast trot. They were obviously trained to trot, Dolf observed, from the rate at which they moved.

"That's some team," he found himself saying.

"I race," the other said, then continued to drive silently and rapidly for several more blocks.

He made a left turn and slowed the team to a walk.

There were a lot of lights here, revealing several saloons, variety theaters, and small restaurants. By contrast with where they'd been, this street was well peopled, with individuals and small groups moving about.

"They won't be coming down this way," the driver announced. "The cops only come over here in platoons. Ever hear of the Barbary Coast?"

"Who hasn't?" Dolf said.

"Yer lookin' at it. Fastest damn Hell's Ten Acres on the globe. Get anything you want

13

here and a lot you don't sometimes. Now —
where was you headed? I'll run you over there
if it ain't across the bay or more'n ten miles."

"I was headed for the Ferry Dock to catch
a hack, but I guess if it ain't too much outa
the way, the Palace Hotel is really where I'm
headed."

"The Palace it'll be. Best in town, although
Lucky Baldwin would skin me if he heard me
say so." Baldwin's Hotel was the Palace's fore-
most competitor.

He drove for a while, then said, "I like your
style. My name's Will Alexander. This is my
burg. Been here since forty-nine. If there's anything I can do for you, look me up. I'll give you
my card when we get to the Palace."

He hadn't asked Dolf's name, and Dolf was
sure he never would if it wasn't volunteered.
But there was something about Alexander that
assured him the secret of the Chinaman, or
any other for that matter, would never come
out of him.

"My name's Dolf Morgette," he said, offering a handshake.

As he expected, he got the usual response.
In this case it was a whistle. "No wonder,"
Alexander said. "I was gonna say that was the
quickest shootin' and straightest in the dark I
ever saw. You are *the* Dolf Morgette, I guess?"

14

"I guess," Dolf agreed. "If you mean the one with the handsome phiz that keeps showing up on the *Police Gazette*, I guess I'm your man," he added, wryly, to allay any suspicion that he might be overly-impressed with his own reputation.

As they pulled up to the Palace, Alexander said, "I ain't sure what you're in town about, but I got a proposition I'd like to talk over with you real soon."

Alexander drove through the arch into the huge courtyard, pulling smartly up to an entrance. A porter appeared almost as soon as the rig stopped. Dolf wasn't surprised to discover that everyone there knew Will Alexander and that he knew them all by first names. Will stayed to see that Dolf was properly accommodated and Jim Too taken care of.

"That dog's a jewel," Will said, as an attendant, after a proper introduction to Jim Too by Dolf, led the huge hound away.

"Saved my life tonight," Dolf said.

"Damn well told," Will agreed. "The Boo How Doy don't often miss."

He noted Dolf's look of puzzlement. "Chinese hatchet man," he explained. "Somebody must want you bad. We better have that talk tomorrow early. I may be able to call the wolves off. How about breakfast here?"

15

"Suits me," Dolf said.

With that they shook hands, and Will drove off at a smart clip.

Dolf had his first ride in an elevator and found the experience a trifle unnerving. A hot tub and a cigar relaxed him. He realized that he was dog-tired. Although he had a lot to consider, he was asleep within a minute of his head's hitting the pillow. He had been pleasantly surprised to discover that Joe had got his trunk to the hotel before him. Hate to have some hairpin knocking on the door at two A.M. to deliver my trunk was Dolf's last thought before he corked off.

# Chapter 2

Shortly after he got up, Dolf noticed a note had been slipped under his door. It read: "You can ring for a bellboy and have the hotel call me when you're up. — Will."

Dolf looked at his watch. It was almost 6:00 A.M. He was an early riser by lifelong custom. With no idea when Will Alexander might ordinarily get up, he decided to call him personally later on. That gave him time for a leisurely soak in a long tub brimful of hot water. The last time he'd had that luxury before coming to the Palace had been at Mark Wheat's mansion in Pinebluff. This recalled a mental picture of Mark's daughter, the beautiful, self-possessed Victoria Wheat, whom he'd once hoped to marry.

I wonder where the Wheats are now? he mused.

He supposed Mark was still a fugitive in

South America or some such remote place. Strangely, he bore the man no hatred, though he'd ruined the Morgettes and, Dolf suspected, had — through his ambitions — indirectly engineered the deaths of Dolf's father and two older brothers.

But he was almost as much a victim as us, Dolf thought. He probably didn't know what a skunk Ed Pardeau was until it was too late.

Pardeau, as sheriff, with his gunslinging deputies, had pulled off the actual killings. Dolf had finally killed Pardeau after Mark Wheat had fled the country. Dolf again recalled his last letter from Mark's daughter stating that she hoped he'd come home.

Almost two years ago, he reflected. I wonder if she's married? Probably is. I wonder too if she'd really have had me like she wrote, after all that happened on account of me.

He tried to dismiss the whole line of thought because it was troubling, but a vague plan to look her up again someday was tugging at his consciousness. The idea kept recurring intermittently while he shaved, dressed, then headed for the elevator. He debated taking the stairs, recalling his distrust of the unfamiliar elevator's wobbling mechanical cage, then thought, I guess I'd better get used to the damn newfangled thing.

He pushed the call button firmly and soon heard the cage clanking upward, its flapping, whirring cables dimly visible in the dark shaft before him. In a while the affair swayed to an uncertain stop at his level. The operator had to jockey it to get it exactly even with the floor and was not entirely successful.

"Please watch your step, sir," he said apologetically as the gridded metal door clanged open.

Dolf had one foot inside just as the cage abruptly jerked upward, then flung himself back into the hall outside. Without his lightning reflexes, he'd have had his head bashed into the ceiling, or perhaps been crushed. As it was, he was thrown to the floor with his nose inches away from the black yawning maw of the exposed shaft, which plunged half a hundred feet to the sub-basement.

He'd caught sight of the look on the operator's face just as the abrupt lurch had started. Had it been startled surprise or sudden calculation? Before he could decide that, the cage unevenly inched back down into the gaping opening and jerked to an uncertain halt. By then Dolf had regained his feet.

"Jeez, I'm sorry, sir," the agitated operator apologized. "We been havin' lots of trouble with this thing. Jeez!" he exclaimed again. "I mighta killed you."

Dolf regarded him speculatively with a poker face.

Was this Twead's first try? he wondered. He could read no duplicity on the elevator operator's face, only apprehension.

"I'll hold 'er steady with both hands this time," the fellow was saying.

"You do that," Dolf said. "Meanwhile I'll take the stairs."

As he walked away, he heard the fellow's pleading voice calling after him, "Hey. I'm sorry, mister. Please don't tell the boss — I'll get canned and I need the job."

"Forget it, son," Dolf called back.

But he himself had no intention of forgetting it. I'll have to look into that young feller, he was thinking. He'd heard there was a class of young punks around big cities that would do anything for money. They probably had police records if they were in that class.

While he was waiting for Will Alexander to come over, Dolf savored a cigar and strolled around the Palace's famous courtyard, watching some early carriage trade come and go. This center court was completely encircled by ornately railed balconies on each floor, which had been provided for guests to promenade around, although Dolf didn't see a single person using them. Probably not very many do, he thought. The first he'd seen stepped out just as that thought occurred to him. Probably a janitor, or something, he idly reasoned, seeing the broom or some such implement in his hand. He was disabused of that notion quickly, however, when the figure threw a rifle to his shoulder and hastily aimed it in his direction. Dolf dodged inside the entry before which he'd been standing. No shot followed.

Didn't get a bead on me in time, he thought. He ducked his head out and in quickly. The rifleman, as he'd expected, was no longer in sight.

He dismissed the notion of calling the police. He hadn't got a good look at whoever it was. Twice in fifteen minutes or so, he thought. He recalled Will Alexander's remark: "Someone must want to get you bad."

Twead? No one else had reason to suspect he'd be in Frisco – or had reason to want to get rid of him, unless it was someone out of his distant past. He suspected that Will Alexander was the sort with connections to get him some of the answers he needed without involving the police. His plans for Twead, if he caught him, didn't involve lengthy and uncertain legal proceedings.

Just then Will Alexander came in. He shook Dolf's hand, saying, "Have a good snooze?"

"First-rate."

"Any more excitement yet?" he asked with a meaningful look.

Dolf grinned. "You won't believe it."

"Shoot, anyhow," Will said.

"Two tries so far, I'd guess. I'll fill you in on the details over a cup o' coffee."

"Keerist!" Will exploded. "We'd better get you the hell outa here."

Dolf told him all about his two close calls while they were waiting for their food.

"I'll have that elevator boy's case looked into," Will said. "I got a place for you to stay with me for a few days, then we can find something safe of your own. Let me handle that. Meanwhile, I got a job that might interest you that could fit in with whatever your plans may be. You ain't told me yet who's so damn anxious to beef you." Then he hastily added, "You understand I ain't pryin'. You don't hafta tell me a damn thing. But if it ain't too private, it might help me find out some things for you."

"No harm in tellin'," Dolf said. He told Will why he'd come to town.

"Twead, eh? I remember the bastard. Couple of gents I know got burned by him for a big roll before he was sent up to Folsom. Well, well. What the hell do you know about that? He probably has friends to hide him out here — but there's a bunch that'll be just as anxious to dig him outa his hole. And if they do, you won't have to handle him personal. Meanwhile, we gotta find you a little more private digs before somebody gets lucky. The crowd that's after you likes to perforate a feller right about where his suspenders cross. Being fast and a good shot don't count against that kind as you well know. Look how Wild Bill got his."

Indeed Dolf remembered how Wild Bill got his, which was not the least of the reasons he'd chosen a seat, back against a wall, as usual. Will hadn't missed that either, nor the fact that Dolf's eyes constantly roved over everything and everyone in the room while they were talking.

Changing the subject, Will came directly to the point. "Got a job you may want — I sure hope you will. Won't interfere a bit with looking for Twead either." He paused, eyeing Dolf speculatively.

After their conversation the previous night, Dolf had been expecting some sort of proposition. As yet he had no idea what sort of business Will Alexander was in, though he suspected he was at least a sporting man, whatever else he might be. He simply waited noncommittally for Alexander to continue.

"You've probably heard of the Big Four." He was referring to the well-known founders of the Central Pacific R.R. Seeing Dolf nod

23

affirmatively, he continued. "Only two of 'em are still left, but I suspect that mealy-mouthed bastard Huntington is tryin' to have me killed." He paused reflectively. "But I don't want a bodyguard necessarily, although it could involve that, too. I need a troubleshooter, and not at piker's wages either — I'll go a thousand a month."

Dolf was barely able to mask his surprise at the amount. A thousand dollars was a small fortune — over two years' wages for common laborers.

"It sounds too good to turn down," Dolf said. "You must really have big trouble. How do you know it's Huntington?"

"Suspicions," Will said. "But damned well-founded suspicions. Someone's been after me, but only since I've started a railroad line headed up north and a ferry service here in competition with the C.P. They're a slick lot, though. On the surface they're friendly as can be, especially that sanctimonious bastard, Stanford. But he may not even know what Huntington's up to. He even panhandled me for a contribution to the damn university he's tryin' to start as a memorial to his son — 'Stanford's circus,' as old Huntington calls it. Huntington, he's the dangerous one. I'd guess he was behind whoever's after me. He runs the Central Pacific almost single-handed from New York. Haven't seen him out here in years." He laughed suddenly. "He's been tryin' to welsh on the bonds the C.P. owes Uncle Sam — convince 'em the R.R. is practically broke. About the time he had Washington all softened up, Stanford bought his wife a hundred-thousand-dollar diamond necklace and probably made the front page of every paper in the world. Huntington goddam near had apoplexy. I wish he had."

Dolf grinned, but largely over Will's obviously huge enjoyment of his competitor's discomfiture. He cared little for money, beyond his modest personal needs, and even less for millions and millionaires. He suspected Will might be one of the latter, but if he was, he certainly didn't fit the public notion of what one was like. Dolf was beginning to feel a genuine warmth for Will Alexander; part of it was his frank manner. The rest was probably his guileless pair of blue eyes that often twinkled over what he was thinking or saying.

"Anyhow," Will said, "we've got to get you out of here. How about letting me put you up at my place — long enough to talk over a deal, and then I can hide you out, sorta?"

With no firm plans anyhow, Dolf thought this was as good a course for the moment as any. After breakfast and checking out, Will drove them up Montgomery Street behind the same team of trotters he'd had the previous night. They turned left up California. Dolf had told Will he had a horse to pick up from the *Alaskan* later.

"We could pick up your horse now if you want," Will said.

"Why not?" Dolf agreed. "You can probably show me a good livery stable."

"The best," Will said, swinging his team into a loping U-turn. "Right behind my shanty in my stable."

On their return, they made an unusual small cavalcade that attracted many eyes, with Dolf's big stallion, Wowakan, pacing behind the buggy and Jim Too following.

"That's Stanford's shebang there." Will pointed out an imposing mansion on the south side of the street. "I live up just a couple of blocks."

The whole area was full of the homes of the rich, a neighborhood still known as Pacific Heights but soon to be known as Nob Hill and a little later Snob Hill. Dolf hadn't believed Will when he mentioned a shanty, but he wasn't prepared for what he found either. He was greatly impressed, not knowing enough about architecture to recognize what might accurately have been described as a "Mid-Victorian atrocity," the typical hodgepodge that borrowed from several historical European styles. Alexander's was somewhat like a French château, three and a half stories of brick, the third story punctuated by ornate dormers, the top half-story mansard with a wrought-iron crown, second story crowded with bow windows and balconies, and the first wholly surrounded by a deep veranda punctured by numerous entrances. Will drove up the circular drive and stopped under a porte cochere. A servant popped out a door to take care of the horses, another to greet Will personally and see to his wishes, if any.

The former "poor boy" in Will showed through as he eyed Dolf for some reaction to this opulence. Dolf grinned a trifle. "Some shanty, I'd say."

Will guffawed and clapped him on the back. "C'mon in. Wait'll you see the rest of it."

Dolf got his next surprise before they were inside. A young lady practically waltzed out the front door, put her arms around Will's neck, and kissed his cheek.

Dolf caught her green eyes speculatively passing over him even as she kissed her father. He noted this with amusement. This was not a typical Victorian woman — and despite her youth she was a woman, tall and willowy, yet generously proportioned — in every sense a nubile youngster, and fully aware of the fact. The green eyes were set in a milky white face framed by deep auburn hair that trailed over her shoulders and far down her back.

Will glowed with pleasure and pride as he took her hand and turned to Dolf.

"This is Diana, Dolf. Dolf Morgette, Diana."

She actually curtsied, much to Dolf's surprise, then offered him a warm, classically formed hand, pressing his with unexpected strength. In the gown she wore, the curtsy had presented a stunning view of quite a lot of Diana for a moment. Just then her eyes had caught and held Dolf's for a brief flicker. Her look unmistakably said, "You've never met anyone like me, have you?"

"Mr. Morgette," she said, "I've heard a lot about you."

I'll bet, he thought. And read a lot more. But he only smiled a little.

Will led the way inside. "May I call you Dolf?" she asked. "You're not gray enough to be a mister yet."

"Sure," Dolf agreed. "Why not?"

He'd almost forgotten Jim Too in the bustle of their arrival, until the big hound came right in with them and proceeded to sniff the strange surroundings.

"I'll get him out," Dolf said, starting back outside and calling to him.

"No you won't," Diana protested.

She knelt and circled Jim Too's neck with her arms.

"What really great eyes he has. So soulful!" she exclaimed. "He's just a big lover."

As though to prove it, and much to Dolf's surprise, Jim Too liberally licked Diana's face. She giggled, pleased as a young boy would have been tussling with a dog.

"I'm taking him out to the kitchen for something to eat," she announced, and disappeared with long strides down a hall, Jim Too willingly following without being coaxed.

"That's Diana," Will said, somewhat amused, then sighing. "There's only one Diana. Now I want you to meet her ma."

Dolf was as unprepared for the missus as he'd been for the daughter. They found her in a drawing room off the long hall, seated before a cheerfully blazing fireplace. The room's warmth was welcome.

She rose as they entered, and Dolf saw a woman who appeared much like her daughter and scarcely older, though he realized she had to be at least forty and probably would be much older. Dolf would have been dumbfounded if he'd known that she was actually fifty-five and had been a prostitute in Hang-town when Will had met her there in 1851 as an eighteen-year-old beauty, during the Gold Rush.

Pioneer California had an old ditty about such commonly understood matings:

> The miners came in forty-nine,
> The whores in fifty-one.
> They rolled upon the barroom floor,
> Then came the native son.

Diana was not exactly a son — and had been born long after fifty-one, of course. She was twenty, born in 1867, almost past her mother's childbearing age and all the more dear because they'd tried so long to have children, sons or not. But they'd really wanted a son. Perhaps realizing that had almost turned Diana into a sort of tomboy — with emphasis on the almost and sort of. They were important qualifiers in her case.

"This is Clementine," Will introduced his wife.

"How do you do," Dolf said, formally.

"Oh my," she said, taking his hand warmly, just as Diana had. "I hope we don't have to go through a formal stage. I'm too damned old to get formal now."

She smiled enchantingly, nonetheless checking to see how the "damned" had grabbed him. To her delight he merely grinned.

"Us Morgettes were never famous for formality," he said. "Everybody calls me Dolf, or worse. I guess you'd like me to call you Clementine."

"Clemmy," she said.

Will watched all this approvingly. He was used to Clemmy and Diana.

He hoped Dolf would get used to his unconventional ladies, because he'd already taken a great liking to him that had nothing to do with expecting anything in return except friendship. However, as he well knew, friendship was the hardest thing for the very rich to come by.

# Chapter 3

Dolf was turning over in his mind his amusing recent encounters with Will's family as he followed him to his third-floor lair. It wasn't quite an office and it wasn't quite a library. Will used it as a little of both, but more as a retreat from the world. The way up was by a richly paneled central stairwell boasting original statuary on fluted pedestals on every landing. It was lighted in the daytime by beveled stained-glass windows, which let in pleasant prisms of light. Their destination was windowed on two sides, paneled in light oak and carpeted with a Persian rug from wall to wall. A battered rolltop desk looked entirely incongruous in the otherwise resplendent surroundings, which included matched sets of books in glass-covered cases along the walls, bound mostly in Morocco or other rich leather. Will eased into a swivel desk chair and indicated a large leather Morris chair to Dolf. He offered Dolf a perfecto, selected one for himself, and leaned back, lifting his feet onto the desk.

"Let's take a load off our feet and confab awhile," he offered.

They both got their cigars going satisfactorily before Will continued. He didn't seem in a hurry to get down to serious business. Dolf knew he had something on his mind but suspected he wasn't ready to spill it just yet.

"What did you think of my family?" Will asked good-humoredly.

Dolf grinned, wondering what he was expected to say. He just shook his head and continued grinning. Finally he said, "I like 'em. Oughta be more womenfolks like 'em."

Will chuckled, pleased. "That's just so. I got a lot better time of it than the rest of the rich dudes up here whose families are always putting on airs."

Finally Will let out a resigned sigh and came around to business. "No point in doin' a lot of jawin' if you ain't in a position to sign with me, but the fact is I sure do need someone like you I can count on. I don't aim to gild the lily. You'll likely earn every cent of that thousand a month. Might not live long enough to spend too much of it either. The crowd I'm up against don't fight out in the open. You got any plans that'd stand in the road of throwin' in with me? And before you answer, you don't owe me a damn thing for the other night, and no one'll ever hear a word outa me about that heathen Chinee regardless."

Dolf didn't have to think over his answer. He'd already decided to give Will any kind of help he needed. His eyes locked with those of the older man. "I'm your hairpin," he said. "I reckon I got a lot of the kind of experience you're lookin' for or you wouldn't have asked me."

He realized that Will could probably do as much for him and his aims as the other way around, and maybe more. However, that wasn't his main reason for deciding. He liked Will Alexander and the man needed help, perhaps a lot more than he showed. He admitted to himself that he would also like to see more of Will's unconventional daughter.

Will's face lit up over the decision. "Good! Good!" He clapped his hands together nervously. "You don't know how tickled I am to hear that. You'll understand why a lot better after you hear what I got to say." He paused reflectively, deciding how he should start. "First you'll have to know something about my business. I got a lot of irons in the fire, some no one knows anything about, not even Clemmy.

Not that I don't trust her. I just don't see any reason to worry her unless it comes down to it. First off, which a few might suspect but not many really know, I make a lot of money down on the coast." Dolf realized he was referring to the Barbary Coast.

"It's rumored that there's a Kingpin who controls most of what goes on down there." Dolf supposed Will's interests were being threatened by some underworld czar. He certainly wasn't prepared for what he heard next.

"That Kingpin is me," Will said, watching Dolf closely for reaction. Dolf was truly taken by surprise. Will, who had expected as much, was pleased to observe Dolf's completely poker-faced acceptance of that information. "I also own a big chunk up on the Comstock that's been profitable for years, but the price of silver ain't what it used to be, though I sure ain't losin' money on the mines. Nonetheless, my real gold mine is over here on the coast. I gotta hang onto that if I'm gonna buck old Huntington and his crowd. They've had a stranglehold on the whole state for years with a monopoly on shipping, even the water routes. Anyone who bucks them gets stepped on good — that is, up till now. My crowd's got just as much money as they have. That never happened to them before. I'm gonna bust their damn stranglehold or die a-tryin'."

Dolf was digesting this information as Will went along. He reasoned that there must be more to it than simply the challenge of making more money. What Will said next confirmed that.

"A few years ago the Big Four decided to welsh on their agreements with the settlers they'd suckered into homesteading along their line down in the San Joaquin Valley. They brought 'em in and settled 'em on land they didn't think was worth a nickel and agreed to sell it at a dollar an acre when the poor saps could afford to pay it, if that ever happened. Meanwhile they held 'em up on shipping for all they were worth. Well, the settlers fooled everybody, maybe even themselves. They put canals over into the Sierras and got water on their worthless land. Today it's like an oasis down there. Naturally the crowd that did the work got so they could pay up with the S.P., or thought they could. That's where Huntington and Co. welshed and jacked the price up and started selling the land to outsiders who could pay a bigger price. You can guess what happened. The homesteaders kicked up a helluva fuss and put up a fight. They got a vigilante committee started and even goosed the U.S. marshal out of there on the end of Winchesters when he tried to throw them off. That's when the R.R. brought in some hired guns. The final outcome was pretty much a foregone conclusion. They couldn't even do anything in the courts, since everybody knows the R.R. controls 'em. There was a big shoot-out down at a ranch that belonged to a feller name Brown. He got killed. So did a bunch on both sides. The R.R. had the newspapers under their thumb and turned public opinion against the grangers. They'd have lost their whole taw except for one thing. Me. Brown was Clemmy's brother — too proud to ever let me help him out — a damn good man. When he got killed, I bankrolled a bunch of his neighbors. Still hold a lot of mortgages down that way. But they're makin' good on every penny I loaned. The point is that I don't forgive and I don't forget. When Clemmy's brother was killed, I made up my mind to gore the railroad's ox damn good. Of course there was no way to tie them in directly — they're too sneaky for that. When the truth finally came through, nobody had any doubt about who engineered the rough stuff. Old man Hearst's boy, Willie, runs the *Examiner* here in town and got so damn mad over bein' bamboozled about the real story, he's been after the R.R. crowd ever since. His old man, George, is one of our senators. He bought Willie the paper as a toy. Me and old George invested in the Comstock at about the same time and have been pretty thick ever since. So I got an ally over at the *Examiner*. The saying is 'Willie warbles, and old George calls the shots.' You can imagine where George stands with Huntington's crowd. Willie has a two-gun writer named Bierce that goes after the Big Four every chance he gets. If they have a little derailment, it ends up sounding like a disaster wiped out half the state. Naturally, Bierce needs them two guns — and everyone knows he ain't afraid to use 'em. They say he cracked his marbles in the Civil War and turned into a mad dog. Personally, I like him. You'll probably meet him one of these days."

The size of Will's game was beginning to be clear to Dolf. The whole U.S. knew that the Big Four ran California and had for years. But the problem with Will's Barbary Coast enterprise still hadn't come out. That he hadn't brought that out seemed to occur to him just then.

He said, "I've been ramblin' around Robin Hood's barn a little here. I may eventually need you out in the sticks when we actually start building the line, but my problem right now is here. Those bastards have found out somehow that I practically own the coast. They've put their money to work with the cops here. As you've probably heard, we've likely got some of the crookedest cops in the country, maybe barring New York or Chicago. The story is they're so crooked they have to screw 'em in the ground when they die." He laughed, and Dolf joined him. "At any rate I've naturally taken care of 'em under the table, but there's always more than one set of 'em. Our problem is gonna be a captain named Hanratty. He's tough, been around since forty-nine and knocked over a dozen toughs or so in his time. He doesn't care which side he puts the holes in either — matter of fact, he'd just as soon have someone else do his work for him. You'll have to watch him every second. Of course, there's no tellin' who's in with him. I'd have bought him off long before now, but in the old days I was one of 'em pullin' on the rope when we swung off his brother. That was in the vigilante days. His brother was a member of a rotten gang called the Hounds. Hanratty told some of us then he'd get even. Made good on a couple of his threats, but he was careful to make it look like self-defense. Maybe it was. If I saw him comin' at me, I'd go to foggin' first if I had a chance. Anyhow, he's managed to get the coast in his precinct. I tried to get him out from the top but somebody greased a lot of palms first —

and for a hell of a lot more than I'm willing to pay. I'd rather fight the bastards. That's where you'll come in. They've been roughing up my joints tryin' to scare people away. It's beginning to hurt, too. But I'm spread out enough that they haven't hurt me too much yet. Some of the galoots that hang out in my joints are as tough as Hanratty's crowd. Nobody is apt to scare them away. They like their red-eye and gals and gamblin'. I got 'em all." He was almost finished. He eyed Dolf for some reaction.

For his part Dolf had seen it all before, only on a smaller scale, in such places as Pinebluff and Ft. Belton. He realized that there was little anyone could do about the accepted aspects of rough frontier recreation. He'd kept order in places that would have given hell a run for its money. The prospect neither repelled him nor caused him any apprehension about his ability to handle the job.

"Well, that's about it," Will said. "I want you to start hanging around some of my places and giving the toughs a dose of their own medicine. What you do about Hanratty is your business. My guess is he won't brace you personally — not from the front anyhow. I know for a fact he thought Shootin' Shep Thompson was the fastest gun in creation. The whole country heard what you did to *him*. You sure ain't gonna have any trouble with Hanratty from the front." He examined the end of his cigar critically, for effect, before concluding, "You still want the job?" He locked eyes with Dolf as he said it.

Dolf returned his stare without expression. "Like I said," he replied, "I'm your hairpin."

"Good," Will said. "I was afraid I might talk you out of it. Tried my best. I wanted to be damn sure you knew what you were heading into. I'll take you down there tomorrow to meet my boys. You may have met a few of 'em before." He grinned, realizing Dolf would understand what he meant, either that he'd run them in sometime or spent some time in jail with them. Everyone, at least in the West, knew Dolf had killed some of Pardeau's deputies in self-defense and had almost killed the sheriff himself and been railroaded to the pen for it. Only after he had been pardoned had he had to kill Pardeau himself, an act applauded widely under the circumstances. By then the truth had surfaced that a Pardeau posse of hired guns had murdered Dolf's father and two older brothers, killings that had triggered the Pinebluff War. That decade-old war had changed Dolf's life, made his reputation as a fast gun, and cut him loose as a wanderer. He didn't seem to be able to break the pattern, though he'd vastly have preferred to go home and settle back down to ranching.

Will changed the subject, saying, "How about lettin' me show you around the rest of the place? By now Clemmy'll have your stuff in a room and be thinkin' about stuffing us with something for dinner. Let's find out where she put you first. Then we can look in on your horse."

"Speakin' of my horse, I'd like to give him a little exercise after bein' cooped up on the ship for a couple of weeks. For that matter I could use some myself. Where's a good place to ride?"

They were interrupted by Diana's voice. "Did I hear somebody say 'ride'?"

She and Jim Too poked their heads into the room at the same time. The dog wagged his way over, nuzzled Dolf, then politely went to Will to find out if he liked dogs. Will gave the big hound a pat and a thorough ear-scratching and head-rubbing.

"I'll show you where to ride after we eat something," Diana said, pursuing her original remark. "I need to get out."

"Suits me," Dolf agreed, looking to Will to see if it suited him.

"Don't look at me," Will said. "My womenfolks do what they damn please regardless of what I think. In this case I'd be all for it if anyone cared."

Diana crossed to him and kissed his cheek. "Oh, Piffle!" she snorted. "Mother and I obey your every whim." She turned toward Dolf and winked broadly.

"Sure," Will said. "So how about showing Dolf where his room is gonna be, and I'll see you two downstairs in a little while."

"Follow me, Dolf, I picked you a room myself. It has a view of the whole town and the bay."

She led him down the hall from where they were and threw open the door to a large sunny room. "There's a back stairs, too, in case you want to be sneaky." She giggled and gave him a sidelong glance that may have meant something, or not. That was what she'd intended it to be. Diana was a finishing-school girl, but no Victoria Wheat, Dolf decided.

"Make yourself at home," she said, coming right in and looking out the window for a moment. It was certainly most unusual to have a young lady follow him into a bedroom, especially when he hardly knew her. "Look," she invited. "You can see for miles. I slept here when I was a child, then I outgrew the space. I've got a suite right below you. But sometimes I still come up here just to sit at the window and look out and dream. I used to dream about a knight scaling the wisteria vines and carrying me off to live happily ever after."

Dolf accepted her invitation to look out. He was a trifle disconcerted to have her step aside, then return to stand very close to him. He was conscious of her skirt touching him and of the delicate cologne she wore. To extricate himself from a situation he didn't understand and that might possibly embarrass him as a result, he stepped away and observed practically, "I don't think the wisteria would hold up a knight in all that armor." He eyed her speculatively for some clue to her thoughts or intentions.

She looked down, then back directly at him. "Anything is possible in your dreams," she said. "Especially when you're a romantic little girl." Then she glided out the door, poked her head back in and added, "Or a romantic big girl." Then she was gone. Her voice, with a hint of laughter in it, drifted back, "I'll see you for lunch — and that ride later."

I'll have to watch my step with that one, he thought. That *is* a fast trotter. Caution was especially necessary because she was Will's daughter. In the first place, he had a code where friends were concerned, and in the second, he counted heavily on Will to help him find Twead. He couldn't afford a misstep that would chill their relations. He suspected that for all of Will's easygoing exterior he could be damned protective where Diana was concerned.

# Chapter 4

After their noon meal, Will, Diana, and Dolf headed for the carriage house at the back of the property. The place encompassed substantial landscaped grounds, though the hill had been barren and windswept when Will had first built there a decade before. "Got the biggest lot up here, much to Stanford's disgust," Will said. "He started with a whole block, too, but he sold half of it to Uncle Mark Hopkins. I miss old Uncle Mark. He was the only one of the Big Four that wasn't a natural-born son of a bitch."

Dolf was a trifle unaccustomed to the kind of language that Will used around his ladies, but he supposed that was how rich city people were. Diana and Clemmy didn't seem to notice. Probably used to it, Dolf reasoned. Of course he couldn't imagine Clemmy's background or what effect that may have had on the latitude she'd given Diana in growing up unconventionally. In time he'd learn.

He was pleased to see Diana saddle her own mount, a tall chestnut gelding. She was wearing the first slit riding skirt Dolf had ever seen, ten years before they became even conditionally accepted. She noticed him looking from her to the man's saddle and back. He hadn't commented on the skirt and didn't intend to. She smiled, noticing the direction of his look. "I designed it myself. Father raised the roof, but I told him it was that or I'd wear carpenter's overalls. The newspapers are still gabbling about it like old women — all except the *Examiner*. Willie Hearst reminds me of a nice proper young girl sometimes, but Bierce gives him some spunk. He thinks I'm the only woman west of the Sierras with common sense — or so he says, and writes. He'll be at the house tonight. What do you think of the skirt?"

Dolf, who was getting used to Diana's strange ways, said, "If it suits you. I could never see how anyone stays on a sidesaddle anyhow."

"Oh I could stay on one all right, but down on the ranch I never figured out how to rope off one, so I started riding astraddle. Up till I was pronounced a young lady, I just hiked up my skirts and rode a stock saddle. When the men began to whistle at me, Clemmy said I'd better stop it. So I designed my own riding out-fit. That didn't get any whistles, but it got a lot of snickers till everyone got used to it."

They led the animals outside, and Diana leaped astride like the born horsewoman she was. Her horse danced nervously, eager to be off. Wowakan tried a few experimental crow hops to feel Dolf out.

"Show off!" Diana cried. "You *let* him do that."

Dolf merely grinned and trotted him back.

"This one bucks, too, if I let him. His name is Henry W. Halleck. Father named him after an old army friend. C'mon," she said, "follow me and we'll go out California to the Cliff House. When it levels off, we can let 'em run."

They rode westward toward the ocean. When they got down the west slope of Nob Hill, Diana urged Henry W. Halleck into a gallop. Dolf let Wowakan have his head and soon passed Diana, who spurred her mount into a run. Hearing the horse overtaking them, Wow-akan broke into a run. Dolf looked back and assured himself she was not gaining on them, though Jim Too was right beside him. He'd have bet Diana thought she had the faster horse of the two. At the end of a mile run, she was ten lengths behind, quirting Henry W. Hal-leck. Dolf pulled down Wowakan to a canter, then, as she drew abreast, pulled him in to a fast trot. He noted the wildly competitive look on Diana's face as she drove past, pulled in her own mount, and circled back. He was expecting some remark, but she rode beside him in silence for several moments. Finally she said, "What'll you take for that horse?"

"Not for sale," Dolf told her. "You can ride him anytime you'd like as long as I'm in town, though." He'd already sized up her riding ability. He'd never seen a woman as good, except among the Indians. She could handle Wowakan, he was sure.

"Thanks," she said, with good grace. "I hate to lose at anything."

"Don't we all?"

"We'll try you again. Henry is out of shape."

"So is Wowakan. Hasn't really been ridden for a couple of years. I had him in Alaska, but he wasn't with me all the time."

"Alaska? I always wanted to see Alaska. Is it all ice and snow?"

"Nope. Gets up to a hundred degrees sometime in the summer up along the Yukon."

She gave him a look that clearly said she didn't believe him, but all she said was, "I want you to tell me all about it sometime."

The moments flew past. Dolf liked to talk to this spirited and unpredictable young woman, or rather listen to her. Talk wasn't his long suit. They were soon past Baker's Beach and heading south along the cliffs. They could see the seals on the rocks below and stopped to watch and listen to them. Jim Too was fascinated by them and tried to work his way down for a closer look. Dolf whistled him back.

"I don't blame him," Diana said. "I love them. They have some at Woodward's Gardens. Sea lions, too. The keeper there lets me feed the trained seals sometimes when no one is around."

Dolf could appreciate that. Diana was the type of woman that men fell all over themselves indulging, he would guess.

"We're lucky today," she was saying. "There's no fog or wind. Look up there to the north. You can see Mount Tamalpais across the Golden Gate."

They rode down past the Cliff House from the north. "We'll come out here some morning for breakfast," she told him. By this time the sun was descending toward the water, where heavy muffled pounding formed a constant background accompaniment. Gulls, crying mournfully, glided overhead frequently. The tangy odor of salt spray pervaded the air. They were riding between the beach and the high rocky cliffs on their left to the east, Diana some yards ahead of him just then.

The bullet ricocheted off his saddle horn with a spiteful whine. Without hesitation, Dolf kicked Wowakan into a run, knowing another might follow almost instantly. He grabbed his reins so the loose ends formed a whip and cracked Henry W. Halleck into a run as he came up behind. "Someone's shooting!" he yelled. "Let's get out of here." The two horses thundered down the beach neck and neck, Dolf scanning the cliffs to his left. He couldn't be sure, due to the thundering surf, where the shot had come from, but he suspected it came from the cliffs, and rode so as to shield Diana from that side. He noted the irate looks of several carriage drivers as they thundered past; no doubt they thought an irresponsible pair was skylarking, needlessly endangering everyone's lives, or at least their peace of mind. Dolf was not sure, due to the surf's noise, whether a second shot had followed or not. After a half mile or so, he reined in Wowakan, Diana pulling up with him. Her eyes were excited, but he could see no fear in them.

"I'm sorry," he said quietly. "Someone is trying to nail my hide to the wall. I shouldn't have risked taking you along."

"Nonsense," she said. "I haven't had so much excitement in my whole life." Then, becoming more serious, she asked, "Who's trying to kill you and what for, or is it none of my business?"

"I'll tell you all about it sometime, maybe. Right now I want to get you home before they make another try. Perhaps you should go ahead by yourself."

A sudden perverse thought captured her mind. "How do you know they're not after me? It wouldn't be very gallant to leave me alone. Maybe I lead a secret life. Besides, Father has a lot of enemies. Maybe some degenerate is trying to get at him through me."

Dolf eyed her to see if she might be serious. She laughed. "You're quite a package," he observed. "I think I'll stick with you and let *you* look out for *me*." But despite the bantering, he kept them at a lope most of the way and was alert for possible danger from any source, including the occupants of passing carriages and the few men on horseback they passed. The sun was low in the west when they regained the Alexander place and turned the two horses over to the groom. They walked to the house side by side. She stopped him before they went inside and looked at him with great, luminous eyes. Impulsively she kissed his cheek.

"I have a big favor to ask. Please don't tell Clemmy and Papa we were shot at by someone."

"Why not?" he asked.

"Because then I might not be able to ride with you again."

He turned that over in his mind. What difference does it make? he thought. Except for no more rides. He wouldn't have liked that either.

"Okay," he agreed.

"Thanks, Dolf. And thanks, too, because you're nice to be with."

Before he could say anything, she led the way into the house.

"Don't forget we're having a party tonight. You'll be the main showpiece. I don't think Papa knew we were having one, but Clemmy is famous for parties. We had this one planned before we knew you were coming, but it couldn't have worked out better."

Despite his protests that he was worn out by his sea voyage and wouldn't fit into the city social affair anyway, and finally that he had nothing suitable to wear — to the latter objection Clemmy pointed out that Dolf was a big man just like Will and could wear one of his tuxedos — Dolf was cajoled into attending the Alexanders' dinner party. He was not sorry that he did. He met Wyatt Earp, about whom he'd heard a great deal, due to the shooting down in Tombstone, and was amused to watch this racing partner of Will's with his reserved, imperturbable exterior and reputation for fearing nothing skillfully herded away from Diana all evening by his dark, voluptuous little wife. Was this fearless lawman henpecked? If so, Dolf thought, it sure didn't keep his wife from looking Dolf over several times so that she was sure he knew she was doing it. Other luminaries at the affair were Willie Hearst; Governor Stanford (as he was still addressed, though he'd been governor during the war); Ambrose Bierce, an incisive, piercing-eyed redhead, now graying — if he wore two guns Dolf thought his tailor merited congratulations; and Lucky Baldwin, a famous sport and multimillionaire womanizer who'd had one or two of them try to kill him after his interest had cooled. There were many other big names. It was an interesting evening, but he was relieved to be able to slip away and turn in.

He hadn't expected anyone to try to kill him in the Alexander house, but he had taken the usual precaution of sleeping with a pistol under his pillow. He cautiously withdrew it when he awoke and recognized that someone had covertly entered his room and was now quietly moving about. He aimed the pistol by sound and held the trigger back as he cocked it, so it would not click while he did so. Then he waited. His surprise was unbounded as the intruder lit a match. It was Diana, wearing only a nightgown. She turned her eyes toward him. He wondered if she were sleepwalking back to her childhood room.

She lit the lamp, turned it low, then faced him. He had been so surprised he still held the pistol in his hand.

"Don't shoot me," she said.

"I thought you were someone coming to have another try at me. You could have been killed sneaking up on someone like me, don't you know that?" he chided her. He slipped the pistol back under the pillow.

"Isn't that lumpy?" she asked.

"What a question. What are you doing here? Is something the matter?" Her presence and the whole situation unnerved him. He was groping for some logical reason for her coming here like this, but couldn't think of a one.

"I want to talk," she said, coming over and sitting on his bed. "I want you to do something for me."

"What?" he asked, still somewhat dazed.

"Pretend you climbed the wisteria."

As she said it, she leaned over and this time very gently kissed his lips, then again, harder and insistently.

He had just presence of mind enough to pull

back and ask, "Are you sure you know what you're doing?"

"Very," she assured him in a whisper, her warm, soft lips caressing his ear.

# Chapter 5

Will's Union Exchange Melodeon was on the northeast corner of Kearney Street and Sacramento. Everyone jokingly called it the Subtreasury, since that famous institution was located just across the street and the Melodeon was almost as popular as if it gave away newly minted gold coins.

"I wanted to locate my headquarters just a trifle off the coast proper," Will said to Dolf as he pulled his team up in front of it. "Get a lot of respectable business that way — the big-money crowd."

Dolf was only half-listening; his mind kept returning to his astounding encounter with Will's delightfully unconventional daughter the previous night. Will had said, "There's only one Diana." Dolf could well believe that now. Yet, despite her breathtaking forwardness, Dolf did not consider her a wanton. He'd believed her parting words, "Please don't think badly of me, Dolf. I admit I'm no angel; I had another affair with an older man, and only one, but it wasn't like this. I knew I wanted you when I first looked at you. I think I am in love with you. Am I making sense?"

He hadn't cared whether she made sense or not. She had drained the loneliness from his life and changed his whole outlook in a few brief hours for which he was grateful. As for love, that could be a two way street. All he was sure of was that no waking moment had passed since then without his mind returning to her. Even at twenty she was as much a mature woman in every sense as he'd ever known.

Will was saying, "Melodeon is a polite name out here for a high-class dive. I've got a regular theater in addition to the usual other stuff. I've had Edwin Booth, Pauline Markham, Lota Crabtree, Eddie Foy, and lots of other first-rate theater people. Right now I've got Minnie Maddern, like the sign up there says. You'll see her some night."

They were entering under an ornate marquee, an area decorated with statuary and potted plants. The building itself was four stories high, heavily ornamented with gothic masonry of several intricate patterns along the eaves and around the windows and doors. The marquee boasted one of the first electrically lit show bills, spelling out with hundreds of small bulbs the name *Union Exchange*. Below it appeared: *Minnie Maddern in* CAPRICE, *Tonight at Eight*. Will kept the marquee lit day and night on the sound premise that "it pays to advertise."

They reached the interior through a bank of eight bronze doors with beveled glass windows in them, curtained on the inside. The first thing that greeted Dolf's eye inside was a deeply carpeted entry foyer banked with mirrors on oak-paneled walls, with paintings interspersed between and a repetition of the statuary-and-potted-plant motif gracing the marquee. Candelabras illuminated the area, spaced between the mirrors and paintings. The ceiling was a high vault, reaching all four stories to the roof. It reminded Dolf of pictures he'd seen of gothic cathedrals, and, in fact, such had been the architect's inspiration. The foyer was even lighted by stained-glass windows high in the front wall, and this subdued light was supplemented by crystal chandeliers pendant from massive beams that crisscrossed above the second-floor level. The second floor itself had a mezzanine balcony opposite the entrance. Dolf had never seen a building so ornate and certainly hadn't expected to hear one called a "high-class dive" by its owner.

Will stopped and regarded Dolf, his expression and stance both obviously asking, What do you think of it?

Dolf grinned. "Some dive, I'd say."

This pleased Will immensely. He said, "C'mon — you ain't seen nothin' yet." He led the way through a set of French doors of rich, dark wood. They led into the theater, a huge room open only in the evening. It was obviously a dinner theater, in which patrons sat at tables rather than in rows of seats. The Union Exchange served dinners and later, during the shows, did an immense business in liquor delivered to the tables by the most highly ornamental, scantily clad young women that could be hired.

The stage was at the far end of the room, currently hidden behind curtains that were decorated with an excellent painting of a formal Roman garden. This room, too, was illuminated by both wall sconces and overhead chandeliers. At this early hour only a few of the subdued side lights were lit, somehow lending a fey realism to the painting on the stage curtains, as though one could walk into the gardens there and be seen no more.

"The saloon's over here," Will said, leading the way through a set of swinging half doors. "We've got a big kitchen over behind it, next-door to the stage. I serve dinner at night. Good as any in town, too. I practically give away the grub and make it up on likker. Of course we make our big dough in the rooms upstairs."

He didn't have to elaborate on his meaning. Dolf recognized this as what it was — a frontier dive on a grand scale, as Will had said, with all that implied. Upstairs would be ladies of the evening and gambling; same old thing, only less obtrusive. In Pinebluff it had all been on one floor, visible as soon as the customer got in the front door.

Will steered him over through the door into the bar. The bar was only lightly patronized at this early hour. A few heads turned, and Will nodded to each, waving to someone at the far end of the fifty-foot-long mahogany slab. Two bartenders were already on shift in anticipation of the influx of trade people soon to be in for "eye-openers" and, later, "bracers," who would form a steady stream all day. The nearest bartender, seeing Will enter, was attentively waiting for him at the front end of the bar.

"Mornin', Stoolie," said Will.

"Mornin', boss." He eyed Dolf briefly.

"I'd like yuh to meet Dolf Morgette. Dolf, this is my head bartender, Stoolie Bong."

At mention of the name Morgette, Dolf noted Stoolie's intensified scrutiny. Will noticed as well and grinned faintly. He'd expected it just as Dolf had. Stoolie didn't have to ask if he was *the* Morgette — wouldn't have anyhow as a matter of etiquette. However, the engravings over the years in the *Police Gazette* and similar sheets had all been good likenesses. Overhearing the name, a couple heads had turned their way from down the bar. It was all an old story to Dolf, seeing eyes studying him so the viewer could go home and describe the "killer" to the old woman and kids. But he didn't get the usual oppressive feeling from it today; instead he thought, Diana didn't care what the hell I was. He was pleasantly surprised to discover that this conviction meant more to him than anything had in a long while.

Dolf accepted Will's invitation to an eye-opener, though he was a very light drinker. Stoolie delivered them both straight shots of good Kentucky bourbon, then politely drew away, pretending to be busy down the bar, in case they were going to talk business.

"Good man, Stoolie," Will said. "Loyal as they come. You can trust him."

Dolf only nodded. He made his own judgments about whom he could trust.

Will, sensing that Dolf reserved judgment, obviously wanted to make his point about Stoolie and continued. "Picked him off the street down on his luck and put him in here. He took right ahold. In a couple of weeks he had the diamond stickpin and cuff links." He laughed gustily. "A friend told me, 'Will, that son of a bitch is stealin' you blind,' but I knew just how much I wanted him to get away with. I told the fellow, 'Hell no, I'm jist gittin' him set up so he ain't a disgrace to the place.' When he got set up, I had a little talk with him and told him just how far his stealin' license went from then on before he went out on his ear. He's been straight with me ever since, goin' on ten years now."

Dolf laughed at Will's remark about gettin' Stoolie set up. It spoke volumes for Will's system of management. He held a loose rein as long as the horse performed.

"Got some people I want you to meet this A.M.," Will explained. "They can't always duck out and come over on a schedule, so we'll have to hang around. Some of 'em may be refereeing a shooting or knifing about the time they planned to leave. There'll be a lot of 'em — each one runs one of my places. I'll give you a list of their names and what they run and the addresses. One o' your jobs will be to drop around to each place as often as you can. If trouble comes up, I want you on call to go like a bat out o' hell to wherever we need you. We can keep in touch by phone. Your horse'll come in handy if you want to use him, or I'll supply you a string of 'em if you prefer. Oh – here comes somebody I want you to get acquainted with. You met him last night – my racing partner, Wyatt Earp."

Dolf had spoken briefly with Earp at the previous night's party and, of course, knew him by reputation as a former lawman and a dead game and honest sport. They nodded to one another now as Wyatt joined them. Dolf, being big and rugged, looked like what he was; Wyatt didn't. The latter was a tall, slender blond with a florid complexion and piercing light blue eyes. His hands were long and slender but strong and callused from handling the reins behind his own trotters. He looked more like a minister than a gunfighter. Dolf had heard he could also scrap with his fists. The calm eyes told it in Wyatt's case; they clearly said, Don't monkey with me!

Will ordered a companion to their own eye-openers for Wyatt, then said, "Let's go to my office. I've got some Havanas that need sampling."

Dolf followed him, Wyatt bringing up the rear. There was a disturbance at the side entrance just as they were filing in. Four policemen in uniform shouldered in.

Will turned, looked, and said out of the corner of his mouth to Dolf, "Hanratty. I expected he might be around looking for trouble. He's the tall, skinny one. Watch him especially."

Will went to meet them, handing something to Dolf as he went. "Put this on," he said. "You'll need it if he's here for what I suspect."

Dolf looked at the metal object Will had shoved in his hand. It was a deputy sheriff's badge. He casually but quickly pinned it to his vest pocket under his coat.

"Captain Hanratty," Will greeted him smoothly. "What an unexpected pleasure." His voice was heavy with irony. "And the Marines. Did you boys get a tip I'm going to be stuck up and come to ride shotgun?"

Hanratty smiled coldly. "Just a routine patrol. The commission is cracking down on the concealed weapons ordinance to put a stop to killings down here. The heat's on us boys over at the precinct."

He approached some of the patrons at the other end of the bar. "I hope you boys understand," he apologized. "It's our job."

His men perfunctorily went through the motions of patting them down for shoulder or back-pocket weapons without eliciting a protest or finding anything. Everyone there who knew Dolf's identity recognized the real objective of the charade.

"Watch the bastards," Wyatt cautioned. "Two of the squad are killers, besides Hanratty."

The captain approached Dolf and blandly asked, "Don't I know you? The face seems familiar." He smiled disarmingly. "I'm Captain Mike Hanratty," he said, offering his hand.

Instead of taking the hand, Dolf set his whiskey glass on the bar and stuck his thumbs in his vest pockets, revealing the star.

"I'm Deputy Sheriff Dolf Morgette," he said coldly. "I'm new here. If you boys ever need any help, feel free to call on me."

He locked eyes with the captain, grinning with his face muscles only. He was pleased to observe Hanratty's surprise and confusion. The captain undoubtedly would have liked to press the matter further but, as Will had said, would be all too aware of what Dolf had handed out to Shootin' Shep Thompson. Hanratty's face reddened slightly, but he lowered his proferred hand with no open show of resentment.

"Glad to meet yuh, Morgette," he growled. "I've heard a lot about you. And the same goes if you need any help."

He glanced at Wyatt Earp, nodded, then silently spun on his heel and called, "Okay, boys, we got a lot more places to cover."

They left by the same door they'd entered. Will came back to that end of the bar grinning. "Score one for the home team," he observed. "Now let's go after those Havanas."

When a string of Will's saloon managers began to show up, Wyatt excused himself. "See you out at the track, I guess," he said to Will. He offered his hand to Dolf. "You run a nice show," he observed, winking. But before he could say more, they were interrupted by loud shouting and a huge crash outside.

A giant braying voice shouted, "I'm boss! I'm chief! I can whip any son of a bitch on the Barbary Coast!" This was followed by another crash and the tinkling of much broken glass.

Dolf glanced once at Will, then stepped out into the saloon with his long-barreled Colt that he used for billy-club cases in his hand, held down at his side. He was alert for an ambush, but only a few bar customers were present, plus the noisy newcomer and two of his friends. The shouter was a man who stood a couple inches above Dolf's six-four and looked to him to weigh at least two hundred and fifty pounds. He had the look of a "pug," with flattened nose and cauliflower ears. He had obviously tipped over a table and thrown a chair across the bar into the liquor shelves.

"Hold it right there," Dolf ordered, loud

enough to be heard as he bore down on the troublemaker. He still kept his pistol down at his side.

The big man lurched around to stare at him bleary-eyed, another chair half-raised to throw. He focused his eyes on Dolf, who would have bet the drunken appearance was mostly acting. His bet was that this was Hanratty's new tactic to harass him, since his earlier ploy to disarm him hadn't worked. If so, he knew none of the three men would be armed. Their game would be to goad him into a brawl on their terms and brand him yellow if he didn't accept the challenge. The tactics never changed; he'd seen it all before.

"Put the chair down," he ordered in a quiet voice, stopping a few feet away.

"Who the hell says so?" the big pug roared, still holding the chair.

"I do," Dolf said, raising his Colt, "and I'll shoot you where it'll do the most good if I have to."

"Hear the big man with the big gun!" the other roared. "I ain't got no gun. Don't need one to hide behind."

Dolf knew what was coming next. So did Will Alexander, who had come out and stood a little to one side of Dolf, followed by Wyatt.

"I know who you are, too," the troublemaker

said in a calmer voice. "You've got the advantage of me. If you think that gun scares me, you're damn well right. But if it was empty, guess where I'd stick it for you."

"Take it easy, Champ," Will interjected. "I sure don't want to see you hurt. Why don't you calm down and we'll talk out your beef over a drink."

"Go ta hell!" the Champ said. "I came to get me a piece of raw meat off this big 'reputation' if he ain't scared to put them guns off."

"Don't do it," Wyatt cautioned in a low voice. "That's Champ Ryan — he's whipped everyone but John L."

Dolf recognized this as well-intended advice. He also knew himself and his record better than they did. The Champ would expect him to either play his game, or stick to his own and keep the advantage of his guns. Doing neither would unnerve the big blowhard to begin with.

"You got an empty room, Will?" Dolf asked.

"Don't do it," Will cautioned. "That's his game."

"Don't count on it," Dolf said. "Here, Wyatt, you hold my guns." He stripped off his coat and peeled off his shoulder rig, revealing a double top-and-bottom holster that still held his short-barreled sheriff's model.

He took two heavy double-barreled derringers

69

from his vest pockets as well. From the corner of his eye, he watched the expression of satisfaction spread across the Champ's face.

"It's your funeral," Will sighed.

"Don't count on that either," Dolf said calmly.

Will produced the keys to a side storeroom, where keg beer was kept. The crowd followed them to the door and tried to press inside to watch the slaughter. Dolf stopped them all.

"Just me and flabber-jabber here," he ordered. "Don't anybody come in till somebody comes out."

As the door closed, Dolf assumed a watchful stance, barely raising his fists.

"Come to daddy," the Champ beckoned.

"Uh-uh," Dolf said. "It's your dance." A picture returned to his mind of a ring back at the Idaho Territorial pen. His opponent had been just about the same weight and mental density of the Champ. The crowd had been roaring for blood, expecting exactly what Will and those outside expected to happen to Dolf. But he'd spent four years then under the tutelage of the shiftiest, dirtiest fighter on the continent, Knucks Geohagan, a boxer, wrestler, and barroom brawler all in one 170-pound package of lightning and barbed wire. Knucks finally conferred his Ph.D. on Dolf: "You're fast as greased lightning. You ain't scared of anything an' you got the killer instinct. Ain't no man around you can't handle if you stay in shape."

And Dolf was in shape. He'd been chopping wood and running behind a dog team for the last year. He'd bet the Champ had been training on beer, whiskey, women, and a lot of good food. He grinned a little.

"I'll wipe that damn grin off," the Champ growled.

He hoisted a swift kick at Dolf's crotch, a move Dolf had expected. He sidestepped swiftly, grabbed the boot at the top of its arc, and propelled the Champ over backward, spinning around and lifting his own boot to the back of the Champ's neck as he went down. He heard the snap of dislocated vertebrae before the big goon crashed to the floor, striking the back of his head so hard it bounced. He was out cold.

Dolf crossed to the door and stepped outside, not even breathing hard and without so much as a hair of his head mussed. Not over a minute had passed since they'd gone inside.

"He'll need someone to throw some water on him," said Dolf unemotionally. He noted the awed looks on the crowd's faces with satisfaction. Running any bailiwick required a certain amount of showmanship. He casually put his guns and coat back on, then approached the Champ's two partners, who were so thunderstruck they hadn't even joined Stoolie and some others who were trying to help their pal. "Who's paying for the busted stuff?" Dolf asked quietly.

One of the pair fished out a roll of bills and tossed it on the bar. "Let Will count out whatever'd square it," he said sheepishly.

Dolf was seated at a table contentedly puffing a cigar and amiably regarding the Champ as they finally helped him out of the side room on unsteady pins. His slightly dazed eyes lit on Dolf and he made an effort to focus them better. Steadying himself, he said, "By Jayzuz, Morgette, yer a good man. Put 'er there." He advanced and offered a handshake. Dolf rose and took the hand, nonetheless on guard for some underhanded trick. Only there was no trick.

"Yez whipped me fair and square," he allowed. "Drinks are on me," he yelled to the house.

Dolf made an exception to his rule and accepted his second of the morning.

"Tell me sumthin'," the Champ asked. "Where in hell'd yez learn that trick?"

Dolf grinned. "Ever hear of Knucks Geohagen?"

The other's mouth fell open. "Knucks! Where the hell is that dirty old son of a bitch?"

"In the pen up in Idaho, unless he's out by now."

"Where the hell did you know him?"

"Guess," Dolf said.

"You did time?" the Champ asked. "Yah, seems to me I heard that. Well put 'er there again. Yer all right. I'd bet on yez agin John L. in a go-as-yuh-please brawl anytime. Maybe even in the ring. D'yaz box?"

"I try," Dolf said.

"C'mon around then," the Champ said. "I'll give yez another waltz accordin' to the rules."

"Match! Match!" yelled one of the Champ's sidekicks who'd overheard the challenge. The word spread that Dolf was going to meet the Champ in the ring, and a brisk round of betting started.

As he was leaving, Champ clapped Dolf on the shoulder and said low-voiced, "Don't expect any more trouble from me outside that ring."

Dolf watched him shoulder through the side door, almost filling it as he passed. Will was smiling at Dolf. "I don't know how the hell you did it, but you hit a good lick there. You've made a good friend. Hanratty put him up to that, but the Champ isn't anybody's man. You can bet it was for money."

"How about putting this in your safe," Wyatt

put in, holding a handful of bets he'd taken on the forthcoming match. "I've got to catch a car for the track." He turned over the money and left, giving Dolf a pat on the shoulder as he went.

"Well," Will said to Dolf, eyeing him across his large mahogany desk, "it's been some morning. I'll have someone scratch up some grub, then I want to show you the rest of my digs here. Later I'll start taking you around to some of my other joints."

# Chapter 6

Dolf had had an interesting and informative day. He would be spending one last night at Will's mansion, then would move downtown to a secluded apartment provided by Will. He'd been conducted around the entire sprawling Exchange environs by Will. Its four stories covered half a block. On the first floor were the dinner theater, saloon, and kitchen, plus several storerooms. A half basement of additional storerooms ran beneath saloon and kitchen. Wide, carpeted stairs led upward from the foyer, giving customers access to the offerings on the second and third floors, above the saloon and kitchen. There were also other stairs behind the kitchen and backstage. The theater extended aloft to the third-floor level; above it, and encompassing the entire fourth floor, Will — being one of San Francisco's leading sports — had installed a gymnasium and boxing ring. Boxing was one of those activities periodically frowned on by pulpit, press, and politicians, so matches were usually conducted in semisecrecy. Since the public disapproval usually only amounted to lip service, in actual fact the times and places of matches were some of the most widely known secrets in town. This public ambivalence explained the relatively secluded location and the popularity of Will's sporting arena. Matches held there were only accessible to the moneyed crowd, who helped assure that the police kept hands off. Another fact of their popularity was that ladies were allowed at these matches and could attend with relative immunity from the customary mock horror of the press, which always appeared surprised over repeated rediscovery that the gentle sex seemed as bloodthirsty as men at these matches.

Will and Dolf had made a cursory preliminary inspection of each of the former's coast properties after touring the Union Exchange. Dolf found many of the establishments' names amusing. There were so many that Dolf made a list of them and their managers' names in a notebook. They were the Bull Run, the Big Dive, Canterbury Hall, Montana, Louisiana, Arizona, Thunderbolt, Cock o' the Walk, Opera Comique, Occidental, Tulip, Brook's

Melodeon, Dew Drop Inn, Rosebud, Every Man Welcome, the Coliseum, and the Latin Quarter. Their managers were an interesting lot – picked, Dolf judged, as much for their fighting ability as for their business acumen. He was surprised to discover that two of them were women – Big Emma, who lived up to her name and ran the Thunderbolt, and Mornet DuMonde, a remarkably attractive young woman with a French accent, as petite as Emma was gross, who operated the Latin Quarter. The latter was not technically a dive, but what was known as a "French restaurant." The restaurant was downstairs.

The personal appraisal given Dolf by Mornet DuMonde suggested to him that she would be pleased if he patrolled the Latin Quarter more frequently than his other reponsibilities.

"Give us the keys to the apartment," Will told her. Turning to Dolf, he said, "I've got something to show you. I think you'll like it." He led the way through the kitchen to a back service area, unlocked a metal-bound door located at one side, threw it open, and stood back to allow Dolf to enter ahead of him. Beyond was a different world. A small foyer, illuminated in the daytime by a stained-glass window, was covered by a rich Brussels carpet of floral design. A carpeted stairway disappeared upward, turning at a landing that was illuminated by a second stained-glass window. Will closed the heavy entry door behind them.

"Got a bar on it," he said. "Just in case a man would like some extra privacy. Those windows have bars on the outside, too. Down in this district it'd be like rolling out the welcome mat to the 'second-story men' without bars on the windows."

He led the way up the stairs and turned on an electric light at the top with a pull chain. "Got gas lighting, too, in case the electricity goes off — and it does every so often." He unlocked a heavy, solid mahogany door on the upper landing and pushed it open. On the far side was a most unusual apartment. The first room was a sumptuously furnished parlor, carpeted in the same pattern as the lower foyer. The furnishings were not the uncomfortable Victorian torture racks currently in style, but Spanish and Moroccan in style, with deep soft chairs and couches. A marble fireplace dominated the far wall, framed by two tall windows hung with heavy lace curtains. The walls were remarkably uncluttered, occupied only by a few paintings, tapestries, and a couple of gaslight fixtures. Above the mantle was a Bierstadt landscape.

"I come here sometimes to relax and think,"

Will said. "Over here there's a bathroom." He opened the door and revealed what was more like a Turkish bath than a conventional American bathroom. The lower walls and floor were done in white mosaic tile set in black mortar. The standard fixtures were accented by a deep, long sunken tub done in the same tile as the walls and floor. The upper walls were papered in a sculptured red floral design. "From France," Will explained, running his fingers lightly over the paper. Pointing to the skylight that illuminated the room through heavily frosted glass, he said, "Bars over that, too. No one's gonna break in here."

Dolf was wondering why Will was taking such pains to show him the place but dutifully followed him through the other rooms, which included a commodious kitchen and a big bright bedroom beside the kitchen with banks of three windows on each of two walls. The bathroom and a big closet were between it and the kitchen.

Will flopped on the brass bed and stretched. "Gettin' old," he grunted, getting back up. "Hate to get up off of it. It's got two mattresses," he added. "Ever try two mattresses? Damn comfortable. The only way to go."

He walked to the windows, looking out both sides. "Not much of a view unless you like beer wagons and delivery carts. What do you think of it?"

"Never saw anything like it," Dolf said. "Got all the comforts home never had." He was unprepared for what Will said next.

"It's yours as long as you're workin' for me — or as long as you want it, for that matter. Good hideout. Not a half dozen people know it's here. Never brought anyone here except the guys that built it and delivered the furniture. Mornet and her brother know it's here. He's outa town most o' the time — works for me on my R.R. project. You'll have to meet him sometime. Big Frenchman. Tough as they come, but dependable."

Dolf hardly heard most of what Will was saying. He was used to living in simple ranch houses or cabins, or sleeping under the stars. He'd been deeply impressed by what he saw, just as he'd been by Will's mansion and the Union Exchange. He looked over the room again with renewed interest. Watching him, Will asked, "Don't you like it? I got others, including one with the gals up on the third floor of the Exchange."

Dolf looked at him and smiled. "Like it? I sure do. It makes the places I've lived in look like barns. It'll take a little gettin' used to — more like a lot, come to think of it."

Will smiled broadly. He'd never forgotten what it was like for a dirt-poor wage slave to strike it rich. He supposed Dolf's mental transition from country boy to this would be just about like his own, despite Dolf's sophisticated grasp of human nature. "We'll move you in tomorrow. Clemmy and Diana said they'd scalp me if I didn't keep you around for supper tonight."

Now Dolf was back in his room at Will's with an hour or so to kill before suppertime. He was lying on the bed in shirt-sleeves and socks, fingers laced behind his head, relaxing and trying to get in focus all that had been happening since he'd debarked from the *Alaskan* four nights ago. The whole thing had a fairy-tale air about it, so pleasant he was uneasy, since every real pleasure he'd ever had in life had soon been marred by violence of some sort. Therefore, his stomach felt a trifle queasy. In addition to trying to assimilate all the opulence to which Will had exposed him — an entirely new world to him, which would apparently be his claim — his thoughts had seldom strayed far from Diana. He tried to throw these thoughts off, sensing guilt at his defection from his not-long-dead wife, Margaret, but had no success. He had loved Margaret desperately, had deeply mourned her and their year-old son who'd died in the flood with her, but time was having its effect. The recollection of how it had been, or even the final horror of it − from the hill above, watching the ice go out and the flooded Sky Pilot River engulf everything, no chance to warn anyone or get there in time − this was too much to hold in his mind. The memory mercifully kept slipping away to be replaced by happier recent scenes.

"Blessed forgetfulness," the words formed in his mind. "People have to go on."

Other thoughts were troubling him. Too busy with Will's immediate affairs, he'd made no progress in tracking down Twead. He had an independent plan of action mapped out in his mind for after he got moved. He trusted Will as much or more than he'd trusted anyone in the past decade, on short acquaintance. But he didn't really know much about him and planned to learn more. He planned in addition some other investigations. First, who had known he was on the *Alaskan* (and how) so that they could arrange the attack on him by the Boo How Doy no more than an hour after he'd landed? Had the same person arranged the elevator accident and the sniper at the Palace? Another thing troubled him. How had Hanratty known so soon that Dolf was with Will and where to find them, at the Exchange at that exact time? Someone had to have been watching either him or Will or both of them. Hanratty himself? Twead or someone in his hire? Maybe both. Perhaps even some other party or parties. He knew his life was on the line every moment he was in this city, and all the more so until these questions were answered. These and the mystery of who had taken a shot at him out by the Cliff House were very much on his mind. The last could only have been Twead or someone hired by him. Or could it? He'd made plenty of other enemies – many of them only recently, in Alaska. Had someone followed him here? He hadn't forgotten Diana's half-joking remark either: "How do you know they weren't shooting at me? Maybe I lead a double life." He dismissed that notion as too preposterous. She was different as he well knew, but not, in his opinion, guileful. She'd been joking.

If someone was after her, Dolf thought, he was a helluva poor shot. Nonetheless, he meant to ask her about that as soon as he was alone with her again. He thought of looking her up right then, but was afraid he'd disturb the household. She herself resolved that.

"C'mon in," he said in response to a light rapping on the door.

She entered quickly, closing the door behind her, turning the night lock and then looking at him. "Don't get up," she said. "I've got you right where I want you."

She smiled, her green eyes dilated and dark under their long lashes as she approached and sat on the bed beside him. She leaned over him and very slowly lowered her lips to his. He didn't move or respond, then pushed her away by her shoulders, smiling up at her.

"I'm glad you're here. But how about your folks?"

"They aren't home just now," she told him. "Besides, they wouldn't care. I told them I'm going to marry you."

He laughed. "And now you're letting me in on it, huh? What did they say?"

"Clemmy said, 'I saw him first,' and Pa said, 'Good. Have you told him yet?' Besides, they both know that I do what I want to. I told Clemmy about last night."

He couldn't believe he'd just heard that. His jaw must have dropped, because Diana giggled.

"You what?" he almost gasped.

She repeated it slowly. "I told Clemmy about last night."

"What the hell did she say?" he exploded.

"She said she envied me."

He gave her a long dubious look, but saw no evidence of evasiveness in her return look.

"By Christ, I almost believe you."

"You'd better. It's true."

He shook his head. "Us country boys aren't ready for the big city, I can see that."

She laughed appreciatively. "Oh Dolf, in some ways you're still a little boy. It's not the city. There's probably not another family in San Francisco like us. I know there aren't any women like me and Clemmy, or if there are, I haven't met any. The rest of the women I know are artificial — all manners and morals — also big shams. Deep down they'd like to be like me. That's why they find so many of them hanging from their chandeliers or with a bottle of gin hidden under their unmentionables. I *know* what *I* am."

He looked at her a long time, then said, "And I like it." He drew her close and kissed her long and gently, then, as she moved beside him, clinging tightly to him, more forcefully. For the moment the notion of interrogating her had somehow fled his mind.

Later, at the supper table, Clemmy looked at them both appraisingly. Dolf wondered what she was reading in their appearance. "What have you two been up to?" she asked with no apparent guile.

"I was showing Dolf the books in the library," Diana said innocently.

Will guffawed. "I'll bet," he snorted.

Despite himself, Dolf grinned. "I'm a great reader," he put in.

Will looked at him. "Yeah," he said. "Of the backs of cards, I'd guess."

"Them, too," Dolf admitted. "Learned from a travelin' revivalist named Shifty O'Doole," he added, poker-faced.

Everyone laughed.

"It'll come in handy after supper," Will said. "We usually play Whist. Clemmy cheats."

"So do you!" Clemmy accused.

Dolf looked inquiringly from face to face to see if they were joking.

Diana came to his rescue. "They're lying," she told him. "We play draw poker. But we all cheat."

That also got a general laugh.

Changing the subject, Clemmy asked Dolf, "Are you wearing a six-shooter under that coat?"

Before he could answer, Will said, "If he ain't, he's a damn fool and I'll send him after one. He's supposed to be bodyguardin' me when we're together."

"I was only going to say if he is, then he's got a good tailor, because I couldn't see the bulge," Clemmy protested.

"It's in his back pocket," Diana guessed.

"Actually I don't have one on," Dolf confessed. "Do you really want me to get one, Will?"

"Naw. If we need one, I got one in my back pocket."

Despite the bantering nature of this exchange, the fact of Will's going armed in his own home revealed that his danger was greater than he'd let on. Nor had Dolf underestimated it. He didn't mention the two derringers in his vest pockets. Technically, however, anyone would have to admit they weren't six-shooters.

The Alexanders hadn't been kidding about playing draw poker after supper. Dolf was glad Will hadn't bragged up his affair with Champ Ryan — and hoped he wouldn't. Will sensed that in Dolf, who had never mentioned it once since. In a couple of hours, during which the talk was all light banter, the Alexanders took Dolf for four dollars at penny ante. Will broke up the game saying, "I guess I'll hit the hay. We gotta get you moved tomorrow."

"Where?" Diana wanted to know.

"Secret," Will said. "None o' yer derned business. Safer for Dolf that way."

"Safer from me?" she asked.

"That, too," Will said.

Diana gave Dolf a you-can-tell-me-later look as she herself left the room. He wondered if she'd be up to see him again so soon. He hoped she would and was not disappointed. With the wonder of her soft warmth pressing insistently against him, he forgot everything else in the whole world and was as happy as he'd ever been. He fell asleep smiling and awoke in the early morning light to see her, awake before him, propped up on her elbow, studying his face seriously.

"I think I'll wear white at our wedding," she said. "What do you think?"

He grinned. "I like what you've got on."

He reached out for her and drew her close. She giggled. "I don't think Willy Hearst would approve," she said. "But he'd sure cover the affair. Bierce would love it. I can see his story captions now: LOCAL HEIRESS IS AWFUL EYEFUL; SPLICED IN THE BUFF. HUNDREDS OGLE. PULPITS THUNDER. STOCK PRICES SOAR. Could we ask for more?" She giggled again.

"You're a poet," he said.

"Poetess," she corrected.

It was broad daylight when she slipped back to her own room.

# Chapter 7

Will had hauled Dolf and his big steamer trunk down to the Latin Quarter in a light delivery wagon he kept for carrying his harness-racing paraphernalia. Wowakan was installed in a stout lean-to stable behind the restaurant and left with Jim Too for company while the two men manhandled Dolf's trunk upstairs inside.

"What the hell you got in this thing?" Will grunted. "Lead?"

"Gold," Dolf said.

"By cripes, I believe that," Will sighed, breathing hard after they'd deposited the steamer trunk in the apartment.

"Matter of fact, there is considerable gold in it."

Dolf briefly filled Will in on the Sky Pilot diggings in the Yukon and his ownership of a good claim there.

"The subtreasury's right across from the

Union Exchange in case you want to cash in your dust."

"Considerin' what you're payin' me, I thought I might keep my gold as a souvenir."

Will laughed. "Your pay's a drop in the bucket. Matter o' fact I was just thinkin' of sweetening the kitty another five hundred bucks a month to get you an assistant. Can't be runnin' around like a chicken with its head cut off twenty-four hours a day, seven days a week. Know anyone who might fill the bill?"

It was Dolf's turn to laugh.

"Sure do. Trouble is, he's probably still up in Idaho."

"Send for 'im."

"If he's out yet. Old Knucks Geohagen would be just the man for the job. I'll check. He must be pushin' fifty goin' on sixteen." Dolf made a mental note to wire up there to find out.

"Well, get whoever you want. Mornet's brother is due to blow in. He could fill in awhile till I need him out in the sticks again. Anyhow, you don't have to start your rounds till tomorrow – get settled in, relax and look around. I don't know as I showed it to you but there's a dumbwaiter in the kitchen." He led the way out there. "They'll send all your meals up. Just put a note on the tray, send it down, and push this button."

As Will was leaving, he turned and said, "The place is yours. Don't feel shy about havin' your dog stay up here." Then he grinned at an afterthought. "Or yore horse either if you can get him up." With that he trotted down the stairs with the spryness of a man twenty years younger than his sixty-plus.

Dolf emptied his trunk and shook out his clothes, hanging them in the closet. Last of all he removed his .45-90 Winchester and leaned it in the corner of the closet.

Some collection, he thought. Forty years and not much to show for it but hopes.

He stretched out on the bed, thinking. The numbing memory of his recent loss of Margaret and baby Henry recurred as it always did when he was alone. He closed his eyes and tried to recall their appearance. His most vivid recollection of Margaret was when she'd saved his life. He could see her bravely diving off the cliffs above Miles Canyon into the torrential Yukon in her foolhardy attempt to save her family. He and baby Henry had been cut adrift by someone while Dolf had been snoozing in the boat, nursing a badly sprained ankle. And she *had* saved them. She had been experienced with white water; he hadn't. I'd probably have drowned us, he thought, recalling his clumsy efforts on the sweep oar till she'd reached the boat, swimming like an otter, to take over the oar. But even being able to swim like an otter didn't do any good at the end, he recalled morosely, the moment of horror vividly flashing back to mind — when she and their baby had been inexorably sucked into the huge vortex where the Sky Pilot river had suddenly plunged under the massive ice jam.

Must have dozed off, he thought when the room later came into focus. Sleep was an escape. For a while he couldn't place the new surroundings or recall how he'd got there. When he did, he lay still and glanced around.

"Funny place for a Missouri farm boy to end up," he said to himself. "Well, this farm boy's got some work to do."

He knew his destination. The day before, he'd picked at random from Will's city directory a firm of private investigators with offices near the Latin Quarter. He'd have gone to the well-known Pinkerton's, except that his prior experiences with them had left a bad taste in his mouth. The outfit he picked was listed simply as "P & P Investigators, satisfaction guaranteed." If he'd known who they were, he'd have gone anyhow, out of curiosity if nothing else. As it was, he was surprised to mount the stairs to the second-floor office in a musty building, push open the frosted glass door with P & P AGENCY lettered on it, and confront an old acquaintance.

"Dolf Morgette!" the man behind a desk inside almost gasped. He lurched up, hands extended as though to ward off a possible attack. Then he seemed to gather his wits. "Hey, Lev," he yelled to someone inside. The inner door bore the inscription LEVERETTE PEEPLES, SUPERINTENDENT. On the outside man's desk was a placard bearing the name O. Pookay.

"You changed your name, I see," Dolf said dryly.

Peeples, exiting from the other office, heard this first, spotted Dolf, then burst into a short laugh. "I made him do it," he said. "Nobody could pronounce it. They all called him Puke."

Dolf grinned. "Seems to me it used to be spelled P-E-U-C-K-E, so I can't say as I blame 'em."

"So what?" the newborn O. Pookay said defensively.

Peeples advanced, holding out his hand. "Glad to see you. I don't know what brings you here, but you're welcome. I owe you Morgettes a heap and won't ever forget it."

Dolf racked his brain, wondering what Leverette Peeples might owe the Morgettes. The first time Dolf had laid eyes on him, Dolf had held a cocked six-shooter at the back of Peeples's head, threatening him. They were out in the bitter winter woods on an Idaho mountaintop. Nonetheless Peeples had been sweating. The last Dolf had seen of these two had been on a stagecoach where two murderous deputies, ostensibly escorting Dolf to a grand-jury hearing, were actually planning to kill him. If either Peeples or Pookay (Peucke) had stepped up to alibi him before then, as they should have, there'd have been no occasion for the grand jury. Their deviousness had almost got him killed in his escape. When the truth finally had come out, they'd both landed in jail themselves for obstructing justice. At the time their roles had been reversed; Pookay, a Pinkerton then, had bossed Peeples, who had been a small-time operator.

"What do us Morgettes owe you?" Dolf asked, seeing no reason to stall and perhaps find out anyhow later.

"Don't you know?"

Dolf shook his head.

"Well, your brother Matt made a deal with me after Obie and me spent a few days in the hoosegow up in Idaho and got out. Matt said I had more sense than someone else, mentioning no names—"

"Bull," Pookay interjected.

"Anyhow, that hundred grand that started the trouble that sent you to the pen in the first place turned up somehow. Matt 'lowed as how I might be able to make a dicker with Wells Fargo to give it back and see that no one else went to jail for it. Figured I might get a reward to boot, provided they got most of their dough back. I got a ten-grand cut and moved down here for my wife's health and hired sweetheart here. Kinda got so's I'da missed him after us bein' cellmates."

"Bull!" Pookay snorted again.

"Besides, Pinkerton fired him an' I couldn't abide seein' a family man starve."

Pookay rallied and said, "To say nothing of the fact that I know more about the business than you'll ever know."

"That, too," Peeples admitted honestly. "So what brings you here, Mr. Morgette?"

"I need some work done."

Both detectives looked expectant.

"What kind of work?" Pookay blurted.

"I'm looking for a man," Dolf said. "But first I need to know something about your clients."

"Confidential," Pookay said smugly.

Dolf gave him an amused stare, cutting his eyes over to Peeples. "All I need to know is who they ain't."

"Fair enough."

"The S.P.R.R.?"

"Nope."

"A fellow named Twead? Forrest Twead?"

"Nope."

"Good. The man I'm looking for *is* Twead. Left St. Michaels, Alaska, for here on a ship a little over a month ago." He gave them the details on Twead and his background, Pookay scribbling it all on a pad on his desk.

"Wadidedo?" Pookay asked.

"Killed a friend of mine in Montana." He told them about Harvey Parrent's murder.

Peeples looked concerned. "What do you aim to do with him if we find him for you?"

Dolf looked blankly at him. "I'm not sure," he answered truthfully. He was a little surprised to recognize that himself. A decade before it would have been a different story. There were lonely mounds all over the Pinebluff district to attest to Dolf's hair trigger then.

"I just don't know," he said again, musingly, as much to himself as them. Then, changing the subject, he asked, "Did Matt tell you where he got all that money?"

"Said he found it hanging in a tree in a sack."

Dolf grinned. "That's the God's truth, too."

"How'd it get in the tree in the first place, though?" Pookay couldn't resist asking.

"Dam'fino," Dolf replied.

Pookay's face mirrored disbelief.

"Besides, you wouldn't believe me if I told you," Dolf said, then added, "Here's where you can reach me." He handed the slip of paper to Pookay.

"This is only a phone number," the other complained.

"That'll have to do. If you want me personally and can't get me there, ask Will Alexander to get a hold of me. I work for him. You know who he is, don't you?"

He needn't have asked, being able to tell by Peeples's low whistle. "Everyone knows who he is."

"You two know anything about him?" Dolf asked.

Pookay averted his eyes, suggesting another question to Dolf. "You guys doing any work for Will?"

"Nope," Peeples answered. "We just know who he is, like I said."

"What's the word on him?"

"You asking as a client?"

"I could."

Peeples thought about that; something about the idea disturbed him. He said, "I don't think I'd care to poke my nose in his affairs for an ordinary fee. Just between us, the word is he's honest as they come, though he's mixed up in the sporting business."

Dolf smiled. "I like the man. Glad to hear that." He decided to drop the subject for the time being. Something in Pookay's attitude had suggested to him that it would be a poor business having them run a background check on Will.

When Dolf returned to the Latin Quarter he found an envelope shoved beneath the door at the foot of the stairs to his apartment. It had an unmistakable odor of cologne about the envelope. He knew whose it was but wondered how she'd known where to find him. He was not surprised she had, however. It read: *Dinner at 7:00 P.M. at the Union Exchange. I'll be chaperoned, darn it.*

*Love, Diana*

He looked at his watch. He had many hours yet. He wanted to exercise Wowakan. After saddling, he mounted, heading through Chinatown, Jim Too dutifully following. He'd heard a lot about Chinatown, but, except for the people, it didn't strike him as particularly Oriental. It was a place of ordinary streets with a greater than average number of overhanging balconies and porches. He intended to pass through and take roughly the same westward course he and Diana had pursued in their previous ride. He even thought of stopping by to ask if she'd join him. This pleasant reflection had lulled his senses, so he was especially startled by a scream followed by an angry shout in one of the buildings he was passing. A Chinese woman darted into the street, running awkwardly. She was soon overtaken by a man, who grabbed her roughly around the waist, wrestling her back the way they'd come. She struggled desperately, breaking away again and starting to run. At this the man drew a long, wicked-looking knife and lunged after her. Just as he reached her and again encircled her waist with a brawny arm, Dolf overtook them both on Wowakan. Not being sure that this wasn't simply a domestic squabble, he didn't wish to see either of them hurt. Rather than "buffalo" the man with a pistol as he might have, he reached down and grabbed his cue, gave the end a dally around his saddlehorn and spun Wowakan into a quick turn. As he'd hoped, the man lost his grip on both his knife and the girl, who spun onto her hands on the ground. Dolf carried the surprised thrashing and yelling Chinaman for several yards, then turned him loose.

He spurred back to the girl. Seeing him coming, she rose and scurried into a nearby building, looking back with frightened eyes. He turned to see what the man was doing, but he had already disappeared. Years of experience flashed a clear warning to him.

"I've been set up," he said half-aloud. He spotted the rifleman on a balcony just where he'd have expected him, down the block the way he'd come. He already had the long-barreled Colt out and answered the rifle shot almost as soon as he heard it. Safer to charge than run, the thought flashed through his mind as he recognized that the first quick shot had missed him. He put spurs to Wowakan, shooting rapidly as he came. He recognized the rifleman's startled face. Twead, by Christ! he thought. He saw his assailant hurl himself through a door behind him, dropping his rifle in his panic.

Dolf leaped off Wowakan, leaving him on dropped reins, kicked open a door, and entered the building at a run, looking for a stairway. There were plenty of doors leading off a long hallway, but no stairs. He rushed through to the back court, a place littered with trash. Here, he took the outside stairs two at a time and crashed through the second-floor door. It looked just like the floor below. He raced down the hall to the front porch. There was no blood, and he'd obviously missed Twead. Reentering the building, he started to look into each room. In the first one that he picked was a woman, absolutely nude. She regarded him with wide, surprised eyes at first, then giggled.

He shook his head in frustration. If Twead's in any o' these rooms, he can stay there, he thought. He'll try again, and sooner or later I'll catch him. I'm surprised the little sneak tried to do the job himself. This set him on a different train of thought. Maybe those friends we thought he had ain't his friends no more.

If that was the case, how did Twead know he'd be riding by there in time to set up a distraction. Or had it been a coincidence of which Twead had taken advantage on the spur of the moment? This seemed most likely. But unless he showed himself again, the chances of finding him if he had Chinatown connections were almost nil. It was rumored that the whole area was underlain by a rabbit warren of interconnecting tunnels as much as six stories deep. But just the same, it could have been a setup, Dolf reasoned. They've got phones here, too. Not hard to call ahead even down here.

# Chapter 8

Dolf found Diana with her parents and the Earps at a table near the stage in the Union Exchange. He was late because he'd called in the police. He relished calling Hanratty's hand on his offer of help. The lanky captain had shown no reluctance, bringing in a detective squad and questioning all the residents and shaking down every room in the house from which Twead had fired the shot, even searching the basement for secret tunnels. Hanratty had apologized over drawing a blank.

"Needle in a haystack," he confessed. "Sorry, Morgette. If I had my way, we'd burn the whole damn neighborhood out and send this bunch down here home — or feed 'em to the sharks."

And that was where the matter rested. If Hanratty had any connection with Twead, Dolf was almost sure he could have detected it in his attitude at some point. All in all, the affair had taken up some three hours, leaving Dolf pressed for time to get home, unsaddle and rub down Wowakan, feed him and Jim Too, bathe, dress, and walk down to the Union Exchange.

"I told Diana you were probably tied up gettin' acquainted with Mornet DuMonde," Will greeted him slyly. "So you needn't worry about an excuse for bein' late. How about some champagne?"

"No thanks," Dolf declined. "How about a brandy?"

Diana eyed him, amused. "Papa also told me what Mornet looks like. Said a dead man jumped out of his coffin one day and chased her three blocks."

Wyatt, whose wife wasn't the sort to relish that kind of railery where her man was concerned, was observing this exchange with the good humor he could afford since he wasn't involved. Just then his diminutive wife asked him with elaborate innocence, "Just what does this Mornet look like, Wyatt?"

"I don't know," Wyatt said, avoiding her eyes. "I've never seen her."

"Looks a lot like you, Josie," Will Alexander said, coming to Wyatt's rescue.

Diana, quickly changing the subject, eyed Dolf reproachfully, saying, "Mr. Earp told me what you did to Champ Ryan. You didn't say anything about it."

"What should I have said?" Dolf asked.

"You could have at least bragged a little," she complained.

Will laughed.

"Less said the better," Dolf observed. "Fighting is Champ's bread and butter. If word gets out somebody took him, it could cost him."

"Already has," Wyatt said, blowing cigar smoke at the ceiling. "Talk o' the town. In a week it'll be all over the country."

"Too bad," Dolf said, accepting the brandy brought by the waitress. "He can thank Hanratty for the whole thing." Dolf neglected to mention his more recent encounter with Hanratty, saving it for when the ladies weren't present.

Clemmy spoke for the first time. "If Mornet DuMonde didn't keep you, what did?" she asked slyly, smiling at Dolf.

"Had my horse out for a run and he went lame," Dolf artfully fibbed. "I walked him back."

"Oh no!" Diana exclaimed. "I'll have our vet look at him for you first thing in the morning."

"Thanks," Dolf said. "Don't bother. Just a cramped muscle. He's out of shape. He almost stopped limping by the time we got back."

Josie Earp had been watching Dolf covertly whenever possible. She was a remarkably beautiful young woman a few years older than Diana. Dolf was sure that Diana noticed her interest in him, too. She had winked at him and rolled her eyes when the others were busy talking.

After dinner, while the ladies were off — probably loosening their corsets — the three men pushed back their chairs, fired up cigars, and got ready for Minnie Maddern's play to come on.

"Wyatt's right," Will told Dolf. "I bet I've taken in a thousand bets already on you and the champ."

Dolf grunted. "I never said I was gonna fight him. That was his pals yellin' 'match.' But I guess there's no way out now. I'll be usin' your gym upstairs to train. Be needin' some sparring partners."

"How about you, Wyatt?" Will asked. "You boxed some."

"No thanks," Wyatt said. "I got a good look at Ryan. I'll referee this one, though, if you'd like."

"Good idea. You're on. Meanwhile, if you know anyone to spar with Dolf, send 'em around."

"Plenty of 'em," Wyatt said. "Some of 'em are bigger'n Ryan."

Dolf eyed Wyatt speculatively, trying to spot some evidence of sly guile in his remark. The other simply puffed nonchalantly on his cigar, but Dolf would have bet his remark about the big sparring partners had been calculated to subtly needle him.

In case that was true, Dolf said, "The bigger the better. All I worry about is they'll fall on me."

The ladies returned before Dolf could get around to Twead's taking a shot at him.

After the show, Will had Minnie Maddern and her leading man join them at their table. Later, as the group broke up, Dolf escorted Diana out to Will's carriage. In the foyer they were treated to the sight of Josie Earp pushing Wyatt outside and heard the tail end of her remark, "As if ogling that Alexander baggage all night wasn't bad enough, I thought you were going to eat Minnie Maddern."

Diana giggled. "Poor Wyatt. Let's wait awhile before we go out. That is, if you don't mind being with a baggage."

"Which reminds me, how did that Alexander baggage know where to send me a note?" he asked.

Her eyes met his, full of mischief. "Promise not to tell?"

"Okay." He was genuinely curious.

"I asked Papa if he'd deliver a note to you since he wouldn't tell me where you were living. Are you going to tell me?"

"Why? Don't you know where Mornet Du-Monde works?"

"No. Papa never talks about that end of his business. But when I find out, I'm coming to see you as often as I can."

"That might not be safe just now."

"Nonsense," she said, sounding miffed. "How are we going to see each other then?"

"I don't know."

"Will you come to see me if I tell you where?"

He regarded her long and carefully. Finally he said, "Yes. But it may be a few days before I'll be free to do it."

"All right," she said. "I'll hold you to that."

Clemmy ducked her head back in about then. "There you are. We thought we'd lost you. Can you come out to the house for a while, Dolf? It's not too late, is it?"

He looked at Diana. "Please," she said.

Dolf suspected Diana had had this scheme rigged with Clemmy, especially when Clemmy and Will excused themselves and went to bed almost as soon as they were home. The last thing Clemmy said was, "If it gets too late, stay here, Dolf. It's getting foggy out.

Streets aren't safe."

"Thanks," he said.

He was still amazed at the equanimity of the Alexanders over Diana's ways, especially Will. It didn't occur to him that Will and Clemmy both really would have been delighted to have him as a son-in-law. Nonetheless, it was true. For his own part, Dolf couldn't imagine how this unsettling situation could possibly unravel itself. But then he couldn't bring himself to believe that Diana, little more than half his age, would really marry him. He simply didn't know what to think about any of them. The situation struck him as almost unreal. Nonetheless, he liked what was happening.

For her part, Diana knew what she wanted. That very morning in a letter to her old school-mate, Victoria Wheat, now living in Washington, D.C., she'd written: *When you come out to visit, you'll meet my wild man. He's really a very gentle and considerate man for all of his reputation. I'm not going to tell you who it is, but I know you've heard of him. And you needn't think you'll steal him with that angelic manner. He's mine and we're going to be married soon.*

Dolf would have been staggered if he'd known of that letter, especially in view of the addressee. At the moment he was trying to rationalize staying another night in his third-floor room.

He finally shrugged inwardly and thought, Oh well, what the hell. To Diana he said, "Would you care to come into my parlor? I expect I've got the same one."

"The Alexander 'baggage' wouldn't settle for less. The lamp is already on low and the bed turned down. I'll see you in a little while."

When he woke up, she was gone. He hadn't heard her slip out.

They were at breakfast when an unexpected visitor arrived. It was Hanratty. He had with him one of the officers who had been with him at the Union Exchange the other day. Will's negro butler announced his presence, and Will went out to see what he wanted. He returned in a few minutes, looking angry.

"What is it?" Clemmy asked, sensing something was wrong.

"They want Dolf," Will said. He looked meaningfully at Dolf. "Some bull about you killing a Chinaman the other night."

Dolf was silent. He'd wondered if that job eventually might be traced to him.

"He wants you to go downtown. I'm goin' along. I'll get my lawyer and have you on the street in an hour. Or would you rather go out the back way while I stall 'im?"

"Let's go," Dolf said. "Might as well find

out what he thinks he's got on me."

"You didn't kill a Chinaman, did you?" Diana asked as he and Will went out. He didn't reply. Diana and Clemmy exchanged worried looks.

"I'll be just a minute and come along with you," Will told Hanratty.

"No need," the captain said.

"I think there is. Let me call my lawyer and have him meet us down at the jail. We'll get to the bottom of this trumped-up bullshit."

Hanratty shrugged, smiling shrewdly. "Suit yourself. We've got an airtight case. Bring two or three lawyers."

Will joined them, and they proceeded downtown in the paddy wagon, no one talking all the way. At the jail they took Dolf's weapons and booked him.

"You want to make a statement?" Hanratty asked. "We've got you anyhow. Found the purser from the *Alaskan*, and he told us you and your dog headed up the way where the China-man was killed. The body had the teeth marks of a big dog in one leg. He'd been killed by a forty-five-caliber bullet. We found two sailors who saw a man answerin' your description headed that way with a big hound just like yours." He grinned over at Will. "Does that sound like a case? Wanna confess, Morgette?"

110

Dolf looked coolly at Hanratty. He grinned a little. "Tell it to the judge" was all he said. He'd seen it all before. Used the technique himself. He'd seen a lot of scared people hang themselves trying to make an alibi with the police.

When no one was in hearing, Will said, "Don't worry. I'll alibi you. Come to think of it, I recall I was waitin' for you just off the dock. Known you for years. Had a confidential job for you and didn't want anyone to know you were in town right off. We went straight to the Palace, right?"

Dolf experienced a great sense of gratitude to this man he'd practically just met, yet owed so much. He clapped Will on the shoulder. "Thanks," he said. "We'll see if I need somebody to alibi me. After all, it was self-defense. Besides, who ever went 'up' in the West for killing a Chinaman? Especially one with a hatchet laying on the ground beside him."

"You ain't aimin' to come clean?" Will asked.

"Hell, no. I ain't aimin' to say anything. Hanratty knows he can't make his case stick with no more'n he's got on me. He just wants to make us fritter away some time. While I'm in court this morning, you'll probably hear one of your joints got busted up."

Just then Will's lawyer showed up.

Will introduced them. "John Gruening, Dolf Morgette."

Gruening sized Dolf up with a shrewd I've-heard-a-lot-about-you look. Will quickly told him what was going on.

"Well," Gruening asked Dolf, "did you kill the damn Boo How Doy? I read in the *Chronicle* about them finding the body."

"Of course not," Will said. "He was with me."

"I asked *him*," Gruening protested mildly. Looking at Dolf, he repeated the question a little differently. "Did you kill the murdering son of a bitch or not?"

Dolf instantly trusted something about Gruening. He told him exactly what had happened without misgivings.

"Good," Gruening said. "Now we'll go over and see the judge and lie like hell."

They told the judge Will's tale. As he'd predicted, Dolf was back on the street in an hour.

Hanratty decided to put the best possible face on it and treat the outcome as a joke. "We may take it to the grand jury anyhow," he said tauntingly.

"Crap," Will said. "You know there ain't no enforceable law in California against sendin' a heathen Chinee to his ancestors, even if Dolf had done it."

Hanratty laughed wickedly. "If? Hell, the shootin' had Dolf's earmarks and the bite had his dog's teeth marks." He guffawed appreciatively over his own joke. "That's two times the Chinese have had a hand in tryin' to beef you, Morgette. Better keep your eyes open."

"What the hell was that about *two* times?" Will asked when they were finally alone. Dolf told him about the incident of the day before. "I really didn't get a chance to tell you before now," Dolf apologized.

"Twead, eh?" Will said. "So he's still in town for sure. I know some dudes'll be damned interested to hear that. Let's go over to the Exchange. I've got some phone calls to make."

When they got there, they discovered what a prophet Dolf had been regarding Hanratty's tactics. A bunch of apparently drunk sailors had practically torn the Latin Quarter apart.

"Insult to injury," Dolf said. "Right under my nose. Only my nose wasn't where it should have been. I need that assistant bad. How about a local?"

"Wyatt might do it for a while."

"Think he would?"

"For me. But only till you can hang around regular. Especially apt to if he can hang around your place. He's got a case on Mornet."

Dolf laughed. As far as he'd seen, Wyatt

had a case on all the good-looking ones. He'd heard about Wyatt's lawing, but the wenching came as a surprise.

# Chapter 9

Mornet DuMonde's account of what had happened at the Latin Quarter didn't make much sense to Dolf. Apparently it didn't to Will either. They'd just hurried over to survey the damage.

"What the hell do you mean, you don't think you could identify any of them if you saw 'em again?" Will asked her curtly.

"You don't pay me for be a bounsair," she shrugged. "I was een the keechen. I hear the racket, look out here, then duck."

She wasn't the ducking kind, as Will knew. He let it pass, merely grunting disgustedly. "What a mess," he said to Dolf. "Let's talk to some of the others. Somebody's bound to have recognized at least one of the bastards."

Dolf was aware that Mornet's eyes were fixed on him often as she ostensibly supervised the help in starting to clean up the mess. He turned to her as Will went off to question the bartender. "Did you call the police?" Dolf asked her.

She shook her head and pointed at Will. "Thee boss says no police onless someone gets keeled. Othairwise, call heem first. So I call heem."

It made sense. In Hanratty's precinct, with him probably behind the violence, what good would police do?

Mornet was a ripe woman. Dolf could see how Wyatt, or any man, might have a case on her. He would judge she was in her early thirties at the oldest. Her skin was as unwrinkled as a young girl's, her complexion olive but with a rosiness seeming to glow through. High cheekbones accentuated passionate, dark, long-lashed eyes. Her generous lips were habitually slightly parted, revealing startingly white, even teeth. A petite yet full-breasted figure with strong ample hips complemented her facial beauty, which was set off by a mountain of long black hair artfully confined in a high pompadour.

"Don't worry, Morgette. We'll be back in beezness eef you wan' deenair tonight." She looked directly at him. "Wy don' you eat weeth me down 'ere? Mornet feex something especial."

"If I'm not out handlin' some more trouble,

Mornet, you've got a customer." He'd heard from Will that the cooking there was fabulous. His small taste of luxury since he'd come to Frisco had whetted his appetite for more.

"Good," she said. Then, looking directly at him, she asked in a lower voice, "You got a woman yet seence you come to Frisco?"

That stumped him. Besides, it was none of her business. He returned her direct look and simply grinned noncomittally.

She laughed with a short staccato release of breath. "I know men," she said. She put a soft finger gently on his lips as she said it, and her eyes turned deep black.

"Tonight," she said. "For sure. Don' deesapoin' Mornet. I wait teel you come." Then she slipped away.

Will had seen this little byplay as he made his way back to Dolf. "You don't waste any time for a man who's almost married," Will kidded him. "Diana'll bean you if she finds out."

"I was more or less attacked," Dolf defended himself.

"Knowin' Mornet, I can believe that." Then he got to the point. "I found a waiter who recognized one of the goons that busted up the place. He's a crimp named Geezer that works over on the waterfront at Grogan's Pub."

Will noted Dolf's puzzled expression and divined the reason. "A crimp's a bastard that shanghais sailors for the ships. Most of the captains get their crews that way. The poor damn sailor gets it coming and going. What we call 'runners' get him to jump ship coming in — and cripes, how they work at that, everything from promises to a gun in their ear. Then they suck him down to some cheap flophouse and keep him drunk till the crimp delivers him back to some captain for a price. Usually they drug 'em to get 'em on board if they don't want to go. Grogan runs one of the worse flophouses right over his joint. I don't allow that kind of crap around any of my places. If you see anything like that going on, bust it up, and don't be gentle. And speakin' of Grogan, I've got plans for him. Let's sit over in a booth and have a shot of something. Time for lunch anyhow."

He called over one of the waiters. "Bring us a couple of my special stock and a menu."

He offered Dolf a cigar. Dolf lit up and waited for Will to proceed.

"You've met Eustace, my butler," Will started. "I asked him if he could find out who's hirin' the toughs that have been tearing up my joints. The word he got is Paddy Grogan, with someone behind him, probably Hanratty, and I know damn good and well who's behind him – the S.P., which is to say that skunk Huntington. A little bird told me old Collis P. is planning a trip out here, by the way. When he does, I aim to have a little talk with him. I want you along when I do."

Dolf nodded. "Suits me. I always wanted to meet a tycoon."

"More like a typhoon in his case." Will laughed. "I hear he's got culture since he moved east. When I knew him, he'd have traded a high-priced painting fer a keg of nails any day. I can hear the bastard now up at his store in Sacramento in the old days sayin', 'Nails keep, horseshoes keep, you other fellers can deal in beans' – he loved nails. Anyhow, I got plans for him if he comes out. Got plans for his boy Grogan even before then. He'll be lookin' for us to hit him back on the off chance we're onto his game. But he won't be lookin' for what I've got in mind."

Dolf looked expectantly at Will but remained silent. Will apparently wanted to savor his plan a little longer. "Let's order some grub," he suggested. Then, changing the subject, he bluntly asked, "You aimin' to marry my daughter?"

Dolf had trouble concealing his surprise at this sudden question. He soberly considered how to answer it and decided another question was his best tactic. "You reckon she'd have me?"

It was Will's turn to be surprised. "Have you? Of course she'd have you. I know my girl. Up till now she's been a terrible flirt with men. I saw that change the other day when she first set eyes on you. Unless me and Clemmy are powerful fooled – and she naturally talks about this sort of thing to her ma – the gal wants you, Dolf. And we want you in the family." His eyes engaged Dolf's directly. "I never met a man I liked any better'n I do you, son. I'd be proud to have you as my son-in-law."

This almost bowled Dolf over. Here was the big question that had been in his mind, being brought to a head suddenly and unexpectedly. He'd thought they probably considered him a sort of barbarian from the sticks, useful and even entertaining as a novelty, but not someone they'd want around permanently. As for Diana, he had no idea what to make of her truly astonishing conduct. He realized he'd figured she was just toying with him till she got tired of the game. He wondered if Will and Clemmy actually knew as much about their relations as Diana had claimed. He knew he had to say something and was racking his brain for just the right words.

"I don't know what to say, Will," he confessed. "For one thing I'm not sure my wife is dead, though I don't see how anyone could have lived through that ice breakup. I saw them get sucked under like goin' down a big drain. We searched for 'em for days. I sorta figured on goin' back after the job is through here and inquiring all up and down the river again on the one-in-a-million chance they mighta pulled through somehow. Sometimes I get a funny feeling that they're still alive."

Will deeply sensed Dolf's anguish at having to go over that subject again and could sympathize with his doubts. "We don't aim to rush you into anything, Dolf. I'm sure Diana doesn't either. And I'm sure you'll do the right thing. I got a hunch it'll all work out fine someday."

After eating and firing up fresh cigars, Will returned to business.

"I got a little plan," he revealed, his eyes twinkling. "I want you and Wyatt to pay Grogan's a little visit, just to make him nervous. Also to look the place over. Here's what I've got in mind. . . ."

Will's plan greatly appealed to both Dolf and Wyatt. The latter insisted on having a snack at the Latin Quarter after he arrived in response to a phone call from Will. "I do a lot better work on a full stomach," Wyatt explained, eyeing Mornet over Dolf's shoulder, where she was still supervising the cleaning-up business.

"You don't say?" Will observed, winking at Dolf. "You never mentioned that before."

Wyatt eyed Will suspiciously for evidence of needling, but the latter was especially busy just then examining the light on the end of his cigar.

It was the middle of the afternoon when Dolf and Wyatt entered Grogan's, standing for half a minute just inside the door and looking the place over. Will had instructed them not to start trouble but, as long as they were there looking around, just to make Grogan as nervous as they could over the possibility that they might start a fight and shoot the place up.

"That's Paddy Grogan himself behind the bar," Wyatt told Dolf.

"Do you suppose he's got a goat?" Dolf asked idly.

"He is one," Wyatt said. "Noted for usin' his head to butt with in a fight."

"Good to know."

Grogan was a tall, coarse man sporting an impressive paunch. As they approached the bar, Dolf could see he needed a shave. A cigar stub was clenched in the corner of his mouth under a black handlebar mustache.

Grogran had recognized Wyatt, suspected

who Dolf must be, and was bracing himself to appear cordially innocent in dealing with them. He didn't succeed. Instead he appeared nervous as they bellied up to the bar.

"Howdy, Wyatt," he greeted them, nodding to Dolf. "What'll it be?"

Wyatt looked at Dolf. "You want anything?"

"How about a beer?" he said, knowing they could nurse a schooner and hang around looking over the place.

"Make it two, Paddy," Wyatt said.

Grogan drew two, elaborately scooped off a lot of foam — by no means his usual custom — then set them in front of the two.

"What brings you down to the waterfront?" he asked Wyatt.

"Showin' Dolf here the town."

Grogan tried to grin amiably. "I don't believe I got your friend's name."

"I didn't say. But it's Dolf Morgette. You maybe heard of him." He was sure Grogan knew who Dolf was.

"Who hasn't?" Grogan said. "It's a real honor to meet you, Dolf." He offered a fat red paw.

Dolf didn't see any way to avoid shaking it.

The place was only sparsely patronized at that hour. Two customers a ways down the bar turned at mention of Dolf's name and stared. They soon had their heads together, and Dolf suspected they would approach him. He was pleasantly surprised when they walked toward Wyatt instead.

"Ain't you Wyatt Earp?" one asked.

Wyatt looked him over, trying to place where he'd seen him before. "You got the right man," he said.

The speaker shoved out his paw. "We met in Tombstone. My name is Luke Starbull. My pard here is Curtis Short."

"I remember you now," Wyatt said calmly — too calmly, as one who knew him would have recognized. "The word's been out that you been tellin' all over the West how you ran me outa Tombstone and have been huntin' me ever since."

Starbull's eyes wavered, and he definitely looked like a fellow who knew he'd put his foot into it and would desperately like to lift it back out. He decided lying was his best bet. "That ain't so, Wyatt."

"Mr. Earp to you."

"Mr. Earp." He said it hastily and tried to smile, but it was a sickly attempt. "Well, I guess I'll be goin'."

"Not so fast," Wyatt said. "As I recall, you was some kind of half-assed detective."

Starbull grinned weakly and nodded affirmatively.

"Hey, Dolf," Wyatt said. "I just recalled that this is the guy rode a horse about eight hundred miles from Denver to Tombstone instead of using the train. Some detective. Did you know there was a railroad connection, Starbull?" He didn't wait for an answer.

This exchange puzzled Dolf. It was the tough side of Earp that he hadn't seen before. It was obvious that Wyatt held a grudge against Starbull, no doubt due to his big mouth, and was venting it as a happy excuse to carry out Will's desire about making Grogan nervous.

"Can you read?" Wyatt asked Starbull.

"Of course."

"Well, if you've been trying to chase me down for a showdown ever since you ran me outa Tombstone, I make the national papers on the average of once a month. Under the circumstances you must be a piss-poor detective if you ain't been able to stumble across my whereabouts in the papers in six years. If you want a showdown right bad, let's step outside."

"Hell, Wyatt – I mean Mr. Earp," Starbull quavered, "I ain't never said any of them things."

Wyatt looked him over disgustedly.

"How about you?" he asked Starbull's friend. "Would you like some cards in this game?"

"Not me," Short said hastily.

Wyatt looked them both up and down once

more with contempt. "Why don't you two light a shuck before I kick both your asses?" Wyatt suggested.

The two hastily made for the door, looking relieved to get off so easily. Wyatt watched them go.

"I shoulda put a head on Starbull for that big mouth of his, but when word gets around how he finally found me, that'll be even worse for his kind."

Grogan had silently watched all this, suspecting just as Will knew he would that Wyatt and Dolf were trying to pick a quarrel as an excuse to shoot up the place.

"Bastards like Starbull burn me up," Wyatt admitted, then said, "I gotta go see a man out back."

He headed for the rear of the place. Dolf knew he would be casing the rear approach. In a while he was back.

"Couldn't be better," Wyatt said in a low voice when he returned. "Lots of packing cases and such out back. They'll suit old Will's scheme to a tee."

The sequel came out in all the morning papers. Basically, the story read about as follows:

Last night, it is conjectured, some gay blades taking advantage of the fact that cattle barges often tie up just across East St. from Grogan's, apparently devised an impromptu set of corral wings leading up to the pub's back entrance. They then herded about one hundred of those famous wild range steers, from the country north of the bay, quickly across the street, up an alley, and into Grogan's back door. At the critical moment they stampeded the herd with shouts and pistol shots. The toughs that patronize the place met their match. One *femme du pave* was seen riding a steer out the front door screaming. Many patrons were trampled, though there unfortunately were no fatalities. Hardly a chair or table was left unsplintered, and several steers that ranged behind the bar absolutely destroyed the liquor stock. One sprightly steer mounted a billiard table and in the excitement left a large calling card on the green cloth.

The word is that Paddy Grogan is breathing fire and plans to have some raw meat if he ever runs down the perpetrators of the foul deed. Sic 'em, Paddy.

Will read this aloud to Dolf and Wyatt where they'd gathered for a prearranged breakfast at the French Quarter. He finished and looked at each of them. "Ain't that a cryin' shame?" he observed. "Whoever could have perpetrated such a high-handed outrage?"

"Search me," Wyatt said, poker-faced.

"Me too," Dolf put in with equal gravity.

# Chapter 10

One thing was clear in Dolf's mind. He had to seriously go into training for his forthcoming fight with Champ Ryan. Champ was no bum. Word got back to Dolf that Champ had gone into training the very afternoon of their first encounter. If he had, he'd likely done so with an awful headache and a stiff neck. This bespoke a man in dead earnest to recoup his damaged reputation. Dolf had taken a liking to the big Irishman and hoped it wouldn't be a grudge fight on the Champ's side.

I'd hate to take a shellacking, he thought, but if it comes to that, he's a mighty good man — I won't have anything to be ashamed of.

Nonetheless, taking a shellacking wasn't the Morgette style. He had Wyatt round him up a couple of sparring partners, Tom Shaughnessy and Joe Beck, both pugs with creditable records. Will found him a tough young fellow with an ambition to box but not a lot of experience yet, Jim Corbett. Meanwhile, Dolf had sent several wires trying to locate Knucks Geohagen, since he'd been released from prison in Idaho. One of them hit pay dirt, so Dolf wired some R.R. fare to Knucks in Philadelphia. Dolf knew there was no better trainer in the business, and probably, despite his age, no better sparring partner.

One feature of the gymnasium at the Union Exchange was a running track entirely around the perimeter, surfaced with a gritty material to enhance traction, and banked on the corners to permit rounding them without slackening speed. Dolf started his training by running on the track daily, then doing sit-ups and working out on both heavy and speed punching bags. Diana insisted on being a spectator during his early exercising periods.

The second day, after watching his running stint, she announced, "I think I'll start doing that, too — tomorrow; I used to be an awful tomboy. Besides, I've got to keep in shape if I'm going to spar with you."

He raised his eyebrows. "Who decided you're going to spar with me?" Dolf asked.

She looked knowingly into his eyes. "I already do," she said softly. Then she put up her fists and made a few playful flourishes under his nose.

He laughed. "Let me warn you about putting up your dukes, young lady. My old sidekick Knucks Geohagen is on his way out here — don't ever make a pass like that at him without warning; he's been at the business so long, he automatically lands one on anybody that looks even a little bit like they may be going to take a poke at him. The same goes for anybody who fights, including my sparring partners. The young ones may be on edge, overtrained, and the old guys might be what they call 'punchy.' Knucks isn't, but some of 'em are. Don't kid around with fighters or you may end up on the deck seeing stars."

She looked dubious, and a trifle displeased at being so obviously lectured. "You sound like Father," she complained.

"For your own good," he assured her.

"I believe you. I'm just not used to you being so serious. I guess we really don't know each other very well." She appeared like a hurt little girl.

Since they were alone, he resolved the slight impasse by drawing her to him and kissing her. When they drew apart, she said, a trifle breathlessly, "That's better."

During the hours Dolf took out for training, Wyatt had taken over making the rounds of

Will's places on the coast. Things remained remarkably quiet for a while. Apparently Paddy Grogan was thinking over the situation. It couldn't have long remained a mystery who had been behind the cattle stampede through his pub.

Everyone sensed, however, that this was merely the calm before another storm. Undoubtedly Hanratty, Grogan, and co. were considering some new tactics.

At the moment Dolf was lecturing Diana, Hanratty was deeply involved in devising those new tactics. The scene was in the sumptuous second-story apartment of the boss of Chinatown, Fung Jing Toy, better known to the popular press of the day as Little Pete. Through his control of the Sum Yop tong — and a political alliance with Christopher A. Buckley, the boss of San Francisco's democratic party machine — Little Pete had become undisputed czar of Chinatown, despite the existence of other rival tongs. He was wise enough to know, however, that his control really depended on the sufferance of the white politicians who ran the city, in and out of government. This put him under the thumb of Hanratty, in whose precinct both Chinatown and the Barbary Coast were entirely located. There were, of course, others besides Buckley above the corrupt captain to whom Little Pete had to kowtow, but Hanratty was currently the front man for all of them, including Buckley. They preferred to conduct their affairs with Chinatown very much sub-rosa. Hanratty couldn't have cared less what anyone thought of how he conducted his affairs. Years of survival around San Francisco's political game and underworld had given him the arrogant confidence inherent in knowing where a lot of bodies were buried. He knew that if his ship sank, he'd take down a lot of others with it. The right people would be damn sure, therefore, that his ship didn't sink.

Hanratty considered Little Pete a great pain in the neck. The Chinaman kept a cage of crickets that he claimed made music, and which he was always expecting others to appreciate. He played the zither. He wrote poetry, and Chinese comedies, which were regularly performed at the Jackson Street Theater, not necessarily because they had merit, but because Little Pete owned the theater. Despite all this, which Hanratty placed under the heading of "crap," he had to admit that Little Pete was useful. He'd arranged the attempt to kill Dolf the night of his arrival in town. Hanratty hadn't been aware in advance that the attempt was to be made. However, in light of Dolf's almost immediate affiliation with Will Alexander, he wholeheartedly approved after the fact. Little Pete had tried to have Morgette killed as a favor to Forrest Twead, an old friend from his days in Folsom prison. Little Pete had been sent up the river before he had learned it didn't pay to brazenly try to bribe white juries and prosecutors. Intuitively recognizing possible future gain, Twead had been almost the only one in the pen who had treated Little Pete as a human being. It had paid handsome dividends. The Chinese had not only arranged Twead's escape, after he himself had served his term, but had just recently tried to eliminate Dolf for him and was now sheltering him. This meeting was the occasion of Hanratty's first sight of Twead. He took an instant dislike to him, which he carefully concealed. One never knew who could be used to advantage. The captain felt that Twead was certainly a potential ally, since he'd shown enough guts (or lack of good sense) to try to eliminate Dolf personally — three times. Little Pete had already told Hanratty privately that Twead had been the rifleman in ambush at both the Palace Hotel and the Cliff House, as well as in Chinatown, about which Dolf had also informed Hanratty the day it happened.

"I think he's berserk," Pete had confided to Hanratty. (Little Pete, raised in the U.S. since he was five, spoke good English and bad Cantonese.) "He's so scared of Morgette it gives him guts. Besides, he was on the 'pipe' the day he tried to gun down Morgette with a rifle, up the street from here. That may be why he missed."

Hanratty had laughed nastily. "Keep him on the 'pipe' then. It only takes one lucky shot. Morgette is the fly in our ointment. We've got to get rid of him sooner or later if he hangs with Will Alexander. Buckley gave me the word."

"The Blind White Devil?" Little Pete almost gasped. He hated Buckley and feared him, at the same time having awed admiration for his power. Like everyone else in his sphere, Little Pete had to pay periodic secret visits to the great presence to pay homage, where the blind Chris Buckley held court in the rear of his Snug Café Saloon. Buckley made the tong leader leave his bodyguards outside, one reason Little Pete resented him. When he'd protested, Buckley had laughed him off. "Hell, nobody'd have the guts to try to kill you here — unless, of course, I put out the word."

This suggestive type of kidding always made Little Pete nervous. Buckley also made the Chinese uneasy, since from his dark world he nonetheless recognized everyone he'd ever met, even once, by their footsteps or handshake. There was no doubt that, out of fear, Little Pete would faithfully have the wishes of the Blind White Devil carried out to the letter whenever possible.

Hanratty himself was not aware that Buckley, in this case, was taking orders from the principal money power of the other major political party — the S.P. Railroad. That was exactly the way Christopher A. Buckley intended to keep it. Word of this kind of deal could queer him with his own party. As a result, Hanratty's knowing too much would put Buckley needlessly in his power.

It had taken a lot of the long green to persuade Buckley to arrange the S.P.'s dirty work. Other than his being a Democrat, he'd also known and liked Will Alexander for a good many years. But enough money had a way of blurring old loyalties. He wouldn't have wanted any physical harm *he could prevent* to befall Will, but he knew of the old animosity between him and Hanratty and wouldn't have been surprised to hear any day that the police captain had finally manufactured a plausible excuse for killing Will. Buckley considered that affair none of his business — just so he wouldn't be the root cause of having Will killed. But Morgette was another matter.

Buckley fell under the heading of an "honest politician" in the facetious parlance of the times, i.e., "a son of a bitch who'd stay bought." The S.P. had bought him. As things stood, Will, principally through Morgette, was in a good position to thwart Huntington's aims. Therefore, Buckley certainly had no objection to Dolf's elimination by any means possible. Dolf was blissfully unaware that, as a result of this, the most potent political force in San Francisco had, figuratively speaking, signed his death warrant. Not that Dolf was ever off guard. The meeting in Little Pete's apartment was taking place because of those dual circumstances. The three present were waiting for Paddy Grogan's arrival. Hanratty was particularly resentful of Grogan's absence, since Little Pete appeared to think he was entertaining them on his zither while they waited. His rendition of "Oh Dem Golden Slippers" was enough to turn its composer (or any composer) over in his grave.

Hanratty had no idea that Pete's atrocious rendition was a deliberate form of needling. The Chinaman deeply resented the fact that the police captain couldn't keep his eyes — and hands, when the occasion permitted — off Pete's special favorite, Heavenly Flower. Before Little Pete had made her his, she'd been a high-paid prostitute, most beautiful and sought after of the girls in Chinatown, and exclusively reserved for the white clientele. Now, even though she was retired (in a sense), Hanratty acted as though she were his whenever he wanted her. Pete was poisonously jealous, but powerless to do anything about it — at least yet. The right opportunity might occur, however.

Grogan arrived just in time to save Little Pete from a defenestration out his own second-story window by courtesy of Hanratty, who'd had as much of the so-called music as he could take.

"What the hell's been keepin' yuh?" Hanratty snapped at Grogan.

Grogan looked startled, ponderously took out his turnip watch and solemnly consulted it. "Nothin'," he finally said. "I'm early, as a matter of fact."

Little Pete, who was perfectly aware of Hanratty's antipathy for his zither, grinned inwardly, behind a very inscrutable, moonlike countenance.

Hanratty did his best to ignore the remark, and his present associates. He consoled himself with the reflection that he was keeping a pretty young thing named Annie over on the coast in an apartment. After 4:00 P.M. he expected to be there in his stocking feet having his first growler of beer. But it was only 2:00. He sighed heavily. Everyone looked to him to speak first. He almost forgot to introduce Twead to Grogan, who was suspiciously eyeing the stranger among them. Grogan didn't trust either Hanratty or Little Pete for two perfectly understandable reasons: No one who knew either of them trusted them, and Grogan himself trusted no one, regardless. It was a rule he figured had kept him alive thus far in some fairly murderous company.

"First of all," Hanratty opened, still glaring at Grogan, "why the hell haven't you been tearin' up Alexander's joints like you started out to do?"

Grogan blurted, "It don't take no genius to figure that out. Nobody in their right mind wants to buck Morgette, or Earp either, or worse yet, both at the same time. Just the look of either of 'em is enough to set a man's arse hole to cuttin' rivets."

"Where'd yuh git the goons that worked over the Latin Quarter?" Hanratty countered. "They did a damn good job."

"That was before Morgette and Earp put out the word. Three of the bastards that were in on that job have signed on since for a two-year cruise as soon as they heard who'd be lookin' them up. Not only that, but none of the three's been off dry land for ten years, I'd bet — that is, up till now."

Hanratty snorted disgustedly. "It only takes one lead pill for them two, just like anyone else."

"That's so about grizzly bears, too," Grogan said. "But bear hunters didn't grow on trees till we got repeaters. In fact they still don't."

"Well, I'll tell yuh this," Hanratty stated coldly. "You'd better find some more goons if yer plannin' to live and do well in this burg."

Grogan shook his head. "I've made me pile. I'm kinda thinkin' o' goin' back home and retirin'." He recognized he was saying the wrong thing before it was half out, the last words trailing away. He glanced nervously at the captain and read a tombstone with his name neatly carved on it in both of the captain's cold blue eyes.

"I wouldn't do that jist yet if I was you," Hanratty said gently.

Little Pete was gratefully taking all this in, since for a change, someone else was on the hot seat.

"We've gotta get rid of at least Morgette," Grogan agreed, trying to get back in Hanratty's good graces.

"Amen," Hanratty agreed. "And I've got an idea how to do it." He looked across at Twead and grinned wickedly. "We gotta get them to come to us. We need some bait."

Twead got the drift immediately. His face registered first confusion, then fear. "Not me," he protested.

"Why not?" Hanratty asked. "You don't have to be in the trap when we spring it. Hell, if I wasn't bein' a nice guy, I'd turn you over to him and he'd probably go home."

That didn't satisfy Twead, but he knew better than to protest. He was thinking of leaving town. Hanratty seemed to read his mind. "In case yer thinkin' of skippin' town, go ahead. It'll git rid of Morgette that way, too, when I tip him off you're gone."

Twead didn't have any place to run to, and he knew it. Besides, he felt a lot safer in the city. He wasn't an outdoorsman. He'd be like a rabbit with greyhounds after him if he ran. He was thinking, Hell, this way I'll at least have someone helpin' me try to get Morgette, why not be bait?

Hanratty went on, "You all probably don't know a crook by the name of Pookay. He used to work for Pinkerton's, but he's always been a crook. I've known him for years. Do anything for a buck. He's workin' for a little agency here in town now. A little bird told me Morgette hired him the other day," he speared Twead with a snide look, "to find you, as a matter of fact." Hanratty laughed his nasty laugh. "Couldn't be better. We coulda given Morgette a blind tip where you're hidin', but he'd have been apt to smell a rat. But he won't be suspicious if his own man gives him the tip-off."

"So what do we do then?" Twead asked suspiciously.

"That's where your old buddy here comes in," Hanratty said, pointing at Little Pete.

"You say — I do," Little Pete said, having learned from Grogan's experience a few moments before.

"If we can't get Morgette some other way and have to bring him down here, I want you to arrange a big fake tong war with a lot of action. In the skirmishing, I want Morgette to get a hatchet in his skull. If Earp comes along, that's his tough luck — he might get the same medicine."

"It'll be risky," Pete said.

Hanratty nodded. "It's a little close to home, I agree. I'd rather get him some other way, but that's one way."

"If it comes down to it, I'll do it," Little Pete agreed. "I owe Morgette plenty. He killed one of my Boo How Doy. The Sum Yop don't forget. Besides, I had to send thirty-five dollars back to his family in China."

"What the hell for?" Hanratty's thrifty nature impelled him to ask.

Little Pete regarded him gravely and said, "It's an old custom. If I didn't do it, the emperor might hear about it and feed my grandfather to the imperial hogs."

Hanratty laughed spontaneously. "You're kidding."

"Nope. I'm not. He'd do it sure as hell."

# Chapter 11

Diana Alexander's going to Pookay as the confidential agent to find her a secret apartment was not simply an unhappy accident or a one-in-a-thousand misfortune. She rather logically selected him, based on what Dolf innocently had told her about the detective. He seemed devious enough to be just the man she wanted. And he was; his only drawback was his connection with Hanratty. How could she suspect that?

Peeples had been out when Diana had visited their office personally. She'd thought of sending the butler Eustace, who had run errands for her since she was a child, but rejected that idea because she recalled his rumored connection to Mammy Pleasant. Many suspected that Mammy maintained an espionage chain of black employees throughout San Francisco, especially among the wealthy, and that she used knowledge gained in this manner for both blackmail and gaining legitimate investment tips. Diana certainly had no desire to place herself in the power of that intriguer, though she'd enjoyed Mammy's performances as a high-paid society fortuneteller at various parties, including Clemmy's. Mammy's midnight seances were the highlight of many soirees given at upper-crust homes.

Pookay wasn't sure who Diana was, and she'd have been wiser to give him an assumed name, although he'd have managed to find out anyhow in time or died trying. However she was new at intrigue and deceived by his "It's the law, ma'am. Nothing will be held more confidential, but I can't take a client without having a name."

The fact of the matter was that money talked in his case. He'd have taken her business if she'd told him she was the Czarina of Russia, especially since everything about her spoke of money. Nonetheless, he dearly wanted to know who she really was, since he was always alert to the possibility of future blackmail.

"My name is Diana Alexander," she finally told him. She knew that few people in San Francisco didn't know that name. But she was far from guileless. "I need a place to work at art. My folks are dead set against my painting — 'daubing,' as they call it. So I want a nice top-floor flat with lots of light and everything for living there sometimes when they think I am out of town visiting girl friends. Oh — and it has to have a fireplace. There's nothing like a fireplace to, uh...dry paintings quickly."

Pookay looked at her straightforwardly but was thinking, I'll bet.

She gave him two one-hundred-dollar bills. "Will that be enough for the first month?" She had no idea she could get the best house in town for half that.

He eyed the roll from which she'd taken them and hesitated. He realized that she knew he saw through her polite lie and thought rapidly. "Better make it another hundred," he said quickly. "Sometimes it helps in a sensitive case. Can't tell how my boss may feel about runnin' the risk of maybe gettin' in trouble with Will Alexander; you are his daughter, ain't you?"

She nodded. Then she pulled off another hundred. She suspected rightly that Pookay's boss would never hear about the deal unless he happened to walk in on it being transacted. She handed Pookay a card with her address. "Send me the keys here in a package. Use the return address that's on the back so they'll think it's something from my girl friend."

Two days later she got the package in the mail. In it were the keys and a note with the address and the added remark: *I explained everything. No one will pay any attention to you.* It was simply signed with the single initial *P.*

Diana had been worried about what neighborhood the place might be in, but had hesitated to be too specific regarding the matter. Obviously Pookay had understood perfectly what was required. It was in a respectable residential area of identical three-story apartment buildings, but not in an area where Diana was apt to run into any of her society acquaintances. It was also the sort of neighborhood where a female pedestrian would not be conspicuous. Diana had a hack deliver her to a nearby store, where she might simply be going shopping, then walked the half block around the corner to her building. Hers was the third-floor flat. She felt as though the eyes of the whole city were on her as she nervously let herself into the entry hall. She was relieved to meet no one on her way up the three flights. The flat was a pleasant surprise, tastefully furnished, light and airy with bay windows overlooking the street, an immaculate kitchen and bath, and two large bedrooms off a rear hall, both with walk-in closets. She returned to the front parlor and tried the gas log in the fireplace, leaving it on and sinking into a large Morris chair.

"Very homey" was her reaction. "My home. Our home. And no one will ever find out."

She might have added, "except Pookay" — and whoever he chose to tell. Nor had the potential of her having stumbled onto him escaped the wily ex-Pinkerton. He wasn't the type, however, to rush out and tell Hanratty who had, in effect, just dropped into their net. Might never tell him. He believed in working all sides of the street. His thought was "Time will tell." Besides, based on past experience, he wasn't about to make the mistake again of underestimating a Morgette — especially Dolf. No telling what Dolf might do to someone on behalf of Will Alexander. He, as yet, had no idea of Dolf's relationship with Diana herself.

Diana was elated at her good luck and could hardly wait to tell Dolf so they could arrange their first meeting at the flat. She still didn't know where he lived and accepted the fact that there could be a reason for him and her father to want it kept a secret. Dolf's main reason for not telling her was that he realized she was willful enough to openly visit him there day or night. He could imagine to what underhanded purpose someone at the Latin Quarter, especially

Mornet, might apply the information that Will Alexander's daughter was visiting Dolf's apartment. In fact, in the case of Mornet, he'd already experienced enough to suspect to what purpose she'd put such knowledge.

He'd returned for dinner with her as promised the night they'd stampeded the herd of cattle into the back door of Grogan's Pub. Dinner with Mornet had been perfect. The aftermath hadn't. Mornet was far from subtle when she made up her mind what she wanted. She wanted Dolf.

After the last of the dishes had been cleared away and Dolf had a cigar lit, she had looked at him knowingly. "I should 'ave 'ad thees meal brought upstairs. We can go up zair now."

He understood her perfectly; any man would have, especially after her similar broad hints that morning. He was embarrassed. Besides, Mornet reminded him of his first demanding wife, Theodora, at least where her conception of men was concerned. He suspected she thought that when a woman — especially one as lovely and desirable as she had a right to feel she was — snapped her fingers at a man, he had no choice but to come running. He also suspected he would risk an explosion if he didn't. What he could say to tactfully avert that was a problem he knew was beyond his limited power with words, yet he had to say something, so quite frankly admitted, "I don't exactly know what to say to that, Mornet." He didn't try to avoid her eyes. She was obviously puzzled but not yet angry.

"Wot you mean, Morgette?" she asked.

He laughed nervously. "I'm flattered. You're a beautiful woman, Mornet." She was beginning to sense evasiveness. He read the change in her face, a slightly petulant look capturing it, causing her lips to droop a trifle.

"You don' want Mornet?" she intoned in a low yet somehow threatening voice. "Is zair some other woman? I don' theenk so. You ain' been in town so long. Watza matter wiz Mornet?"

"Nothing," he protested honestly.

Another thought captured her mind. "Watza matter wiz *you*, then?" She almost sneered.

He sighed heavily, recognizing the futile dead end down which this conversation was doomed to proceed. Inexperienced as he was with very many women, he was old enough to have had this happen before. Women almost universally complained that men were after just one thing. If they found one who was not, it became obvious that they actually preferred the old, comfortable robbery regardless of what they said. Further, much as they complained of the faithless nature of men, they were never prepared to accept a man protesting that he was married as a suitable excuse for being rejected. Knowing all this, Dolf, half-humorously, decided to employ that dodge anyhow.

"Mornet, I'm married. I do like to be with you. I hope we'll be friends."

He could read her reactions to each of these statements in the changing expression in her eyes and slyly relished them while displaying a deliberately guileless face. In chronological order, he'd bet her reactions to each statement were, What difference does that ever make to a man? So what? And who wants to be?

She didn't even try to smile. "Okay, Morgette," she said. "I'll be your frand." But her eyes put the lie to that. He recalled the old saw "Hell hath no fury like a woman scorned."

Especially a woman like Mornet, he thought. I'd better start eating someplace else unless I want rat poison.

She stalked away without once looking back. He went out the front to avoid meeting her again, then slipped around to the back entry and let himself into the apartment stairs. Just as he went in, he caught her watching him from a slight crack in the kitchen door. He grinned and thought, I'll bet she has someone sit up all night to see if some other woman slips upstairs.

He surely hadn't made a friend; far from it! Unfortunately, his past experience warned him that in a situation such as this one, that could be very bad.

Will innocently added the crowning touch to Mornet's displeasure. He'd taken up the habit of meeting Dolf and Wyatt for breakfast at the Latin Quarter for strategy meetings, although strategy didn't seem to be necessary just then.

"Things have been remarkably quiet," Will was saying as they put down the last of breakfast and got to coffee and cigars. "Too damn quiet I'm afraid. I should have hired a couple of guys like you two even sooner. By the way, Wyatt, I know you want out as soon as possible – Mornet's brother is due back soon. He can fill in till Dolf's pal Knucks gets to town. Knucks sounds like just what we need."

Dolf added, "He's just what I need right now, too, with less'n a month to get in shape. Old Champ is really out to put a head on me, I hear."

Wyatt was paying small attention to the talk, being more interested in following Mornet's movements as she bustled around playing hostess and supervising the employees. She'd made a great show of paying a lot of attention to Wyatt and ignoring Dolf, much to the latter's amusement. She had given him one haughty glance, then never looked directly at him again.

"By the way, Dolf," Will said, "Diana wanted to get in touch with you."

"I can drop by," Dolf suggested.

"Won't be necessary. I hope you don't mind, but I told her you're staying down here. Didn't see any harm in it since it's a mortal certainty Hanratty knows — and probably by now most anyone who wants to knows, including Twead if he's still around."

Dolf considered that, then shrugged. "It's okay. I haven't tried to sneak around. Better to let Twead have another try at me. I keep my eyes open." He paused. "Is Diana plannin' on droppin' around?"

"I invited her and Clemmy down for a late breakfast. They should be along any minute. We can have some coffee with 'em."

Dolf noted Wyatt's heightened interest at the mention of Diana. He liked the ex-lawman a lot and was inwardly tickled over his weakness for the ladies, which Wyatt thought no one noticed. Almost everyone had, especially his wife, who had an eye for a good-looking man herself.

The ladies arrived shortly, and Will had them all moved to a large table at the rear of the establishment. Mornet, like most women of her type, regarded all women as rivals, especially attractive ones. Diana and her mother were certainly that, since Clemmy looked years younger than she was – in fact, some people took her for Diana's older sister or a young aunt but, unless they knew, never her mother. Wyatt, who was gallant if nothing else, narrowly avoided breaking the furniture, china, or his ankles, trying to help both women to their seats.

"Thank you, Wyatt," Clemmy said, smiling and batting her long lashes.

All this escaped Will, but Diana and Dolf exchanged winks, a fact instantly noted by Mornet, who was hovering nearby with menus. This small intimacy, suggesting something more than a casual acquaintanceship, placed all of Mornet's senses on alert. One did not have to watch Diana for very long when she was around Dolf to realize that he had done something to her that she had liked a lot. Recognition of this set Mornet to seething inwardly. She didn't care that Diana had seen him first. What Mornet wanted she wanted against all odds. She narrowly restrained herself from slamming down Diana's menu. As she hastily withdrew, she threw Dolf one poisonous narrow-eyed look that no one noticed, including him.

So that's the way the wind blows, Mornet was thinking. But the realization didn't absolve Dolf of anything in her eyes.

The crowning blow came when the group broke up, all the rest leaving while Mornet overheard Diana tell Clemmy, "I'll be along later. I want Dolf to show me where he lives."

Mornet was definitely disconcerted to see that neither Clemmy nor Will seemed to show the slightest objection to such an unconventional suggestion. Wyatt reacted, but he didn't count at the moment. Any other time Mornet would have set her cap at once for a man as handsome and interesting as Wyatt. But she'd become obsessed with Dolf, largely because he seemed impervious to her normally irresistible charm despite her unmistakable overtures. She was in a mood to make him regret it. To add insult to injury, Dolf took Diana through the kitchen to the back entry. Mornet considered the kitchen her private domain and didn't once stop to think that Diana probably could own the whole place if she asked her father for it.

Mornet was in this poisonous mood when Hanratty dropped in somewhat later. She normally disliked the lanky, long-nosed Irishman with his pale blue eyes that seemed to see everything and look right through people. In fact, he'd been after her shortly after she'd come to work at the Latin Quarter, before Will had made her manager, and she'd had an awful time keeping away from him till he finally gave it up. Since then she'd been tolerant of him, recognizing what his political clout could do to harm her business. This morning he said, "I hear you got a celebrity livin' here now."

She merely raised her eyebrows and looked puzzled. He tried again. "A famous man. Morgette."

She shrugged. "Oh, zat one. So what?"

Hanratty sensed something here. He tried another ploy. "Lots of people lookin' for him. Ain't you afraid your place might get some bullet holes in it with him sittin' around here?"

She looked at him disdainfully. "Who cares? I don't care eef ee gets bullet 'oles in eem."

Hanratty laughed, as much to give him time to turn that over in his head as anything. Then he ordered breakfast, but he resolved to pump Mornet some more about her attitude. After breakfast he was quite direct. "Sit down, Mornet," he said. "I wanta talk to yuh." There was nothing unusual about a precinct captain and the manager of a French restaurant getting their heads together. Everyone knew the restaurant was a cover for what was conducted more profitably upstairs. It didn't prevent the Latin Quarter from being one of the best restaurants in town.

Hanratty eyed Mornet narrowly and came directly to the point. "I take it you don't much care for Morgette?"

Suspicious, she didn't say anything. She knew which side her bread was buttered on, and all about the old animosity between Hanratty and Will. Finally she said, "Suppose I don'?"

"What'd he do to you?" Hanratty asked bluntly.

"Non o' yor damn beesness!" she told him.

"But you don't like him?"

She remained silent, but the message was clear.

"How'd you like something to happen to him?" Seeing her alarmed look, he quickly added, "Nuthin' that'll hurt him permanent. Just take a tuck in his sails and get him outa our hair for a while." He used the word "our" confidentially and deliberately. She didn't seem to notice.

Their heads were close together for several moments. She didn't like or trust Hanratty, but Mornet was the type of woman who demanded revenge for any slight, if it could be had. She didn't see where she had anything to gain by patience in Morgette's case and in fact had almost no patience in any case.

"Eeet's a deal" was the last thing she said to Hanratty. "Mornet weel let you know when.

You do thee rest, eh?"

"I'll do the rest," the captain assured her as he swaggered out. He started whistling at the door and was smiling narrowly. He had to admit to a grudging admiration for Morgette, but the man had picked the wrong side. He savored the thought of the opportunity his probing remark to Mornet this morning had opened up as a possibility. Yes indeed, he thought. We'll get him outa the way for *a while.* A long while. What Mornet doesn't know won't hurt me.

He actually chuckled out loud. Buckley had put the pressure on him plenty. He felt a lot better over the present prospect of getting it off.

# Chapter 12

Mornet DuMonde was an unusually complex person. Her agreement with Hanratty had left her emotions in seething conflict. She even burned her hand as she helped Marcel, her luncheon chef, by boiling some water. She made a few eloquent French remarks, which he wisely chose to ignore, instead quickly providing a pan of cracked ice and insisting she hold her hand in it, then later greasing it gently with lard. She thanked him with a grateful look, then went into the corner and sat pensively sipping a cup of tea. Her problem was that she really didn't want Dolf hurt and didn't trust Hanratty. For all of her petulant femme fatale airs, she had a generous heart. As an example, when she had learned that her Uncle Henri Lemoine had been executed in Canada, she had wept on and off for days, remembering how he had held her as a baby, had tried to fend for her as she grew older in a bruising world that seldom understood her impetuosity as he did, and had finally written her one last loving letter of advice about life, while in the shadow of the gallows. He hadn't been her blood uncle, but everyone had called him Uncle, and he'd tried to be an uncle to anyone in need, which had undoubtedly got him killed. Her brother and his followers had tried to break him out of jail and spirit him away to the U.S., but had failed due to the extraordinary precautions taken by the mounted police guarding him. She also knew she would cry for days if anything fatal happened to Dolf, yet she wanted to humble him and suspected she would go through with her agreement with Hanratty in the end. She knew herself and her vanity all too well.

Therefore, when Dolf sent down his usual evening request for dinner, she was ready. She telephoned Hanratty as soon as she sent the order up in the dumbwaiter. It had included a request for some bones for Jim Too. She smiled as she selected them. Mornet liked animals. She especially liked Jim Too. As soon as she had discovered Dolf was keeping him out in the stable with Wowakan, she had insisted he allow her to bring him in occasionally. She always fed him and talked nonsense French baby-talk at him, which he seemed to understand, if no one else did. He'd follow her sedately into the kitchen, tail wagging, and was allowed to flop down and snooze there, out of the way under the big salad-cutting table.

Her summons brought over Hanratty quite soon. He took a table in the restaurant. Grogan and his crimp Geezer joined him shortly. When Mornet came over, Hanratty asked, "How long does the stuff take to work?"

She shrugged. "I don' know. Maybe 'alf hour. Maybe sooner. Depends on 'ow moch coffee ee drink. Maybe ee don' drink any," she said slyly, shrugging again.

"You got a key?" Hanratty asked, ignoring her jibe.

"Sure," she said. "We geet een easy if ee din' bar the door."

Hanratty swore. "What the hell would he do that for?"

She merely shrugged again and went back to the kitchen. "We wait," she said over her shoulder.

That morning, after Dolf had taken Diana upstairs to see his "digs," she had insisted that they take a hack over so he could view and place his approval on their new flat. After a predictable interlude, they'd then driven over to the Union Exchange, where Dolf planned to put in a couple of hours training. True to her threat, Diana had taken up running on the track there daily. She was starting to do sit-ups and working with dumbbells as well, much to the consternation of Dolf's sparring partners. The two older ones weren't quite sure they should approve this gross breach of custom. Jim Corbett was enchanted. He filled Diana with blarney whenever he thought Dolf was out of hearing. She wore her slit riding skirt and a blouse for exercising, which Corbett dubbed her 'knickers and weskit.'

After working out, Dolf had sent Diana home and taken over the patrol down on the coast from Wyatt. He returned to his apartment near dark, pleasantly tired and hungry. He stabled Wowakan and took Jim Too upstairs, where he'd been letting the dog spend nights with him. He didn't bother barring the door, since Jim Too would be an excellent alarm system if anyone tried to sneak in. After a soak in the long tub, Dolf sent his note down for supper. He didn't want to run into Mornet till she had a chance to cool off a little. He smiled at the recollection of the cold shoulder he'd got that A.M., and even more so when he recalled how he'd caught her spying from the kitchen door as he and Diana had departed after only a short tour of his apartment.

"Bones for you, too," Dolf told Jim Too as he made out their supper request. The hound raised his ears, looking attentively at Dolf as though he understood the words. Dolf then lit a cigar and sunk into one of the big, comfortable chairs in the parlor while they waited. He was reflecting on the startling speed with which the pace of his life had picked up since getting acquainted with Will and his operation. Basically, deep inside, he was not happy with this fast whirl. The one bright spot was Diana. He recognized that he had a very soft spot in his heart for her, if he was not falling in love, and he wasn't entirely certain about that. He knew all the reasons why it wouldn't be right. Her youth, the possibility that Margaret was somehow still alive, the fact that Diana was rich and from a wholly different world — and it all counted for nothing when he reflected that she appeared to love him and was mentioning marriage.

Why not? he asked himself. I'm not the type to be single. Few men are. After one more shot at Alaska to look for Margaret, why not?

But he truly hoped that perhaps some miracle had kept her and Henry from what had appeared to be certain death. He had even envisioned them picked up by Indians and kept from communicating by some accident, or simply by the vast distances of the country itself.

Jim Too had already attuned himself to what the sound of the dumbwaiter meant. He could hear it coming up as soon as it started, so the buzzer activated from below was actually superfluous. He was waiting with tail wagging by the counter where it came up before it got there. Dolf gave him his bones on newspapers spread on the floor and patted his head as he went to work on the first one. He reflected that it had been only a little over two years since he'd given the gangling, half-grown and half-starved pup a sack of bones back in Pinebluff. He'd just been pardoned from prison and the pup had been the first new friend he'd made. In fact, he'd been one of the few friendly presences in the old hometown. Since then they'd become inseparable.

Dolf laid his own meal out on the kitchen table. Being from cattle country, he started with a large mug of hot coffee with cream and sugar. His tastes were simple, running to steak, potatoes, gravy, and pie for dessert. It was what he'd ordered every evening, with a big pot of coffee so there'd be enough to have with his after-dinner cigar.

When he'd finished, he returned to the big

chair in the parlor, carrying his cup of coffee and feeling pleasantly relaxed. He pulled off his boots and propped his feet up on a hassock. Only later did he sense that he was not only unusually relaxed but also seeing things a bit blurred. He rubbed his eyes and had trouble moving his arms to do it. Then he realized what the truth was.

Drugged, by damn, he thought. He knew what to expect next, and realized he didn't have much time. He forced himself to get up and out into his kitchen to the telephone, staggering almost uncontrollably. Gotta call Will, he thought. No one else I can trust.

His legs were rubbery. The operator kept asking, "Number, please. Number, please." But he couldn't seem to focus his mind on Will's number. Finally it came to him. It came out slurred. "What number did you say, sir?" the operator asked.

"Fiffy doo," was the best he could get out. He could hear some number begin to ring and prayed it would be the right one. Also that some member of the family would be home. The help might not understand his grave peril, or even try very hard to understand what he said, for that matter. He fought to keep from falling off his chair or collapsing head-down on the table, and was barely successful. After what seemed a long, long time, he heard an answer.

"Hello."

He couldn't speak, his mouth feeling full of something choking him.

"Hello."

Don't hang up, he prayed. Finally he managed to lisp, " 's Dolf. Tell Will I'm drugged. Need help."

"Dolf," he heard the voice coming from a vast distance. It was Diana. "I'm here alone," she gasped. "Where are you? I'm coming."

He couldn't force out another word. The last thing he heard was Jim Too's fierce growl. He dimly realized what that probably meant. He wished he had barred that door. Then he simply went to sleep, sprawling disjointedly onto the floor. After that he remembered nothing.

Diana had to calm herself and collect her wits, but the panicky thought, My God, what can I do? crowded out clear thinking. The realization that Dolf may have fallen into the power of someone who would kill him overwhelmed her rationality. She sat down, shook her head angrily, and dug her nails into her palms.

I've got to try to be calm and think like I've never thought before, she told herself. But she felt the numbing panic gripping her again. Anger came to her rescue. I'm not going to put up with this goddamn nonsense! she thought.

She had no idea where her father and mother were. The police, she knew, would be no help. It was Hanratty's bailiwick if Dolf was at his apartment, which he probably was. Then she thought of Wyatt Earp. He might be at home. She hurriedly scanned the list of telephone numbers Will kept by the phone. "Here it is," she said to herself, vastly relieved.

Mrs. Earp answered the phone. "Is Mr. Earp in?" Diana asked, breathlessly.

There was a silence at the other end. "Who's calling?" Mrs. Earp asked cooly.

Diana tried to keep herself from becoming angry. "Diana Alexander," she said, exasperated nonetheless over this inane delay.

"And what might *you* want with Mr. Earp?" The voice had become decidedly chilly and hostile.

Diana drew a deep breath, her heart rising higher in her throat. Suppose this insanely jealous woman hangs up, she thought, in panic. She managed to say quickly, "Dolf Morgette just called for Father; he isn't home. Dolf could barely talk. He said he'd been drugged and needed help. I tried to find out where he was, but he wasn't able to say anything else. I think he must be at his apartment. If Mr. Earp is home, he can get there before I can get any other help."

"Have you called the police?" Mrs. Earp asked, exasperatingly.

Diana almost swore. She tried to hold her temper, realizing that precious time was passing. "It's Hanratty's precinct. I don't have time to explain, but he's apt to be the one that had Dolf drugged. Mr. Earp will understand. Please let me talk to him." There was a long silence on Mrs. Earp's end; the fact that she liked Dolf and that this wild tale might be true made up her mind. Finally she said, "I'll call Mr. Earp to the telephone."

Thank God, Diana whispered inside.

When Wyatt came on, she hastily told him what she knew. "He's probably at his apartment over the Latin Quarter," she guessed.

"I'm on my way," Wyatt told her, and hung up.

Diana cursed Mrs. Earp's jealousy. Even seconds might have been vital. She had no intention of sitting on her hands waiting for someone else to save her man's life. She hastily scrawled a note to her father and left it pinned on the coat rack where he invariably stopped on his way in. Then she grabbed the shotgun he kept in the front-hall closet, checked it to see that it was loaded, and headed for the stable. She lit the gaslight inside the stable door, quickly bridled Henry W. Halleck, and crawled on him bareback, using a saddle rack to step aboard from. Last, she reached down for the shotgun she'd leaned against the wall and guided the big horse out the door into the night. Outside she kicked him into a gallop, balancing the shotgun across his withers. Those on the streets who saw this improbable apparition, wildly clattering past under the gas streetlights, probably suspected they were seeing things – a woman riding astraddle in a flowing skirt, long hair flying behind, galloping bareback at breakneck speed down California Street, juggling a big gun before her.

Mornet unlocked the door to the stairway and cautiously crept up, peeking in Dolf's door to discover whether he was unconsious yet. Jim Too growled and advanced to attack, being aware that something serious was wrong with Dolf. He recognized Mornet's voice as she assured him, "Eet's all right, babee. Eet's Mornet."

That settled him down. He followed her as she cautiously approached the kitchen door and looked in, seeing Dolf sprawled on the floor. The sight almost changed her mind about going through with this thing. Finally she slowly returned to the stairs and called down, "Eet's okay. Ee's out like a light."

Hastily Grogan and Geezer rushed up the steps. Jim Too didn't like that. He advanced, growling. Grogan pulled out a pistol.

"No," Mornet yelled quickly. "Don' shoot. I geet eem in thee bedroom an' lock thee door."

This she was able to manage because the big hound trusted her. But as soon as he discovered he'd been duped, he set up a frantic barking, lunging at the door and threatening to break his way through it.

"*Vite! Vite!*" Mornet urged the two crimps. "Geet eem out of 'ere!"

They took Dolf's limp form between them, hardly able to handle his weight, especially since he was relaxed. "Christ, he must weigh a ton," Grogan gasped. "Why don't we just beef the bastard here?"

Mornet's eyes narrowed dangerously. She pulled a small pistol from somewhere under her skirt and placed it against Grogan's temple. "Geet out!" she hissed. "I might 'ave know I couldn't trust zat bastard Hanratty."

Grogan was afraid to turn his head, stopping in his tracks and dropping Dolf. "Hey," he yelped, "I was kiddin'. Hanratty told us jist to put him on a ship for a little cruise. That's all we're gonna do. He'll have me beefed if I don't."

Mornet looked uncertain. Then she agreed. "Okay. But you 'urt heem an' I keel you myself."

She put the pistol away. They hustled Dolf down the stairs like a sack of potatoes. Mornet checked to clear the coast for them to the rear entrance. Upstairs Jim Too was still creating a deafening racket.

Gabriel DuMonde, the name he now went by, was a legend in Canada's prairie country. He was a huge bear of a man, strong as an ox, desperate as a wounded tiger, and known wherever he had lived as a man not to be trifled with. He had just arrived back in Frisco by the Oakland ferry and trudged the few blocks to the Latin Quarter to tell his sister Mornet he was home and to get something to eat. Since it was the short route, he approached up the alley from the rear. He was just in time to see the tail end of Dolf's abduction — a prostrate form being hustled into a light wagon by two men. He made nothing of that. It was a familiar scene on the coast, one that its habitués were hardened to. If a man spent all his time rescuing improvident sailors from being forcibly recruited back to sea, he'd have no time for anything else.

When Dolf finally started to come around slightly, he could see stars dimly overhead and feel a rocking motion. The air was cold and smelled of salt spray. He could hear oars being plied in a set of oarlocks. Then he heard words that he tried to unscramble; they were more like a distant ringing than a real voice. He could make out, "Where's the goddamn ship? We can't be rowing around here in the dark all night."

"Hold your shirt on," a second voice said. "Can you tell if he's still out?"

"How the hell would I know? It's too dark to see."

Dolf tried to move and discovered that his hands were bound together behind him. Have to get loose somehow, he thought hazily. It really didn't seem too important, though. He was still too sleepy and soon passed out again. When he next awoke, he was still being rowed somewhere in the same boat. He'd only been out a minute but it seemed as though it had been a long time.

"I see the damn ship, I think," a man's voice said. "Off to port. Pull that way."

Being shanghaied, by damn, the thought painfully dawned on Dolf. And it doesn't look like there's much I can do about it.

# Chapter 13

Dolf and Knucks Geohagan knew one another pretty well after spending five years in the pen together. For that reason Knucks arrived on foot carrying his bag to the Latin Quarter. Dolf knew that if he wired more than R.R. fare and eating money, Knucks might have ended up in the Sandwich Islands or Cairo, rather than San Francisco. On the other hand, Knucks knew that unusual things had a habit of happening where Dolf was concerned. Therefore he wasn't too surprised to be almost stomped into the ground by a galloping horse wildly turning into the alley beside the Latin Quarter, or to see it lose its footing and fall in the mud, throwing a young lady who'd been carrying a shotgun which flew through the air as they fell. He gallantly helped her to her feet. She didn't seem unduly damaged, only slightly disheveled and muddy.

"Are yuh hurt, young lady?" he asked, incongruously removing his hat, ceremonially bowing, and adding, "Knucks Geohagen at yer service, ma'am."

"Oh, thank God!" Diana gasped. "You're Dolf's old friend. He's in terrible trouble."

I never knew him when he wasn't, thought Knucks, but he didn't say it. He did say, "What's the trouble, young lady?"

"Follow me," she said, retrieving her shotgun. She briefly and breathlessly told Knucks about Dolf's phone call as they sped down the alley to the rear of the place. Shortly after they were out of sight, a hack galloped up to the front and Wyatt Earp leaped down, hitting the deck at a run. "Wait there," he yelled back at the driver and headed through the front door.

This all happened no more than five minutes after Gabriel DuMonde had arrived. He was in the kitchen with his sister Mornet. After giving her a bear hug and a kiss he'd said in French, "I'm hungry. How about a bunch of buffalo ribs?"

She gave him a look. They'd been raised on them. "Ah, how I wish we had some. How about some cow's ribs?" she said, speaking in their native French.

He shrugged. "It'll do." Then he noticed the dog barking incessantly upstairs. "What the hell's that?"

She hesitated. "If you don't tell Will Alexander, I'll tell you."

It was his turn to hesitate. Will Alexander had been very good to them both. And Gabriel knew his sister's ways. "You've been up to something. Spill it," he ordered.

She said, "Will put a notorious gunman up there. I've been having trouble with him."

She told him what she'd done, trying not to sound or look guilty. "What Will don't know won't hurt us."

"Who was he?" Gabriel asked suspiciously.

"His name was Morgette. You've probably heard of him."

"Morgette! Dolf Morgette?" Gabriel exploded.

She nodded, recognizing that something about what she'd done was just about to backfire.

"You goddamn fool!" Gabriel exploded. "Morgette is my friend! He risked his life trying to save Uncle Henri with me!"

Her eyes widened, then tears quickly came to them. "Oh my God! I really didn't want to do it."

"How did Morgette bother you?" Gabriel asked. "That doesn't sound like him."

She tried to avoid his eyes. He knew her like a book and instantly drew the right conclusion. "It was the other way around, wasn't it? And he wouldn't have you because he's married?"

Before she could answer, Wyatt burst into the kitchen, noticed Gabriel, and said, "You're back. Good. I may need you." To Mornet he said, "Where's Morgette?"

Gabriel told him. Just as he was finishing, Diana and Knucks burst in from the rear and heard Gabriel say to Wyatt, "Dat bastard Grogan'll have Dolf een a Whitehall boat by now."

Everyone there knew what they meant. Whitehall boats were the famous conveyances used by the crimps to carry shanghaied sailors to ships anchored out in the bay.

"Wyatt," Diana said. "Thank goodness *you're* here. This is Knucks Geohagen. Maybe we can catch them yet."

Wyatt was one of the best men anywhere for a situation such as this, right in his element; his mind functioned like clockwork under pressure and he was undoubtedly among the finest men at generalship that had ever worn a star. He didn't hesitate for a second.

"I've got a hack out front. Gabriel, you and Knucks c'mon along. We'll hit Grogan's Pub first. He isn't the kind to be out in a Whitehall boat himself. But he'll know where that one is headed if we catch him and make him squeal.

We'll take the bastard with us."

None of the three men protested Diana's tagging along still packing the scattergun.

At Grogan's Wyatt ordered, "You two take the back. I'll go in the front." Remembering Diana, he ordered "You stay here with the hack. We may need it again."

She watched Wyatt disappear through the batwing doors. Suddenly she was cold and started to shiver. She was scared, too. The hack driver, who was tickled over the excitement to which he'd drawn a front seat, had been watching her, wondering if he dared ask what the devil was going on. He noted her chill and handed her down a horse blanket. "Take this, ma'am. You'll feel better."

There was a sudden racket inside the pub, with yelling and a loud crash. Suddenly Grogan was propelled through the front door by Knucks, who had a hammer lock on him. Wyatt followed, yelling "The first snoot out that door gets a hole in it." He waved a six-shooter to emphasize his point. Anyone who knew who he was — and that included everyone on the Barbary Coast — was not about to stick his head out very soon.

The little cavalcade headed straight across East Street toward the waterfront, which was just at the far side. Diana ran to join them.

They went down a stairway illuminated by a gaslight, Diana bringing up the rear beneath her blanket, still carrying her father's shotgun. Wyatt noticed her and was about to send her back, then thought of how a young woman would fare alone at night in this district. "Get in," was all he said, pointing to the big White-hall boat.

Grogan started swearing again, and Knucks bore down on his arm harder. "Shut up," he grunted, "or I'll break yer wing."

"Don't do that," Wyatt cautioned. "He won't be able to row this thing."

"I ain't rowin'," Grogan protested.

The click of Wyatt's pistol cocking next to his ear changed his mind. "You'll row," Wyatt said. "And you'll find Geezer and the ship he's headed for, too, or we're feedin' you to the fish."

Grogan got busy with the oars. "I'll take the other set," Knucks said. Very shortly it was obvious he knew how to use them. Inside of a few strokes they were in the swell, the lights of shore slowly bobbing up and down. The dong of a distant bell buoy could be heard occasionally, the only sound other than the splash of the oars and the gradually diminishing voices, laughter, and music from the saloons along the waterfront. The night was dark but unusually clear, with only an occasional low, wispy cloud chasing across the stars overhead.

"How much start did they have on us, Grogan?" Wyatt asked close to his ear. Grogan hesitated a second too long and netted a cold round gun nozzle in the back of his head.

"Only a few minutes," Grogan rasped quickly. "Jeezez. Move that thing away. Yer thumb might slip."

"It might," Wyatt agreed.

After several minutes of rowing, Wyatt said, "Stop a minute. We'll look around and listen."

The chill air helped clear Dolf's head; that, plus appreciation of his peril. He tested the binding on his arms and found no slack or stretch in it. He cautiously felt around for something sharp that he might cut it with but discovered nothing. There seemed to be only two men with him, both rowing. It was dark enough that his movements down in the bottom of the boat were concealed. He carefully rolled slightly to one side to try to fish the jackknife from his pocket and had the satisfaction of finding he could work one hand in. After working at it for a few minutes, he discovered that they must have frisked him and relieved him of his knife. That scotched his only chance of getting an even break for escaping overboard. He realized that if he was going to try that he'd have to swim with his hands bound behind him. It was a desperate chance to take, but he had no intention of finding himself on a two-year cruise of the seven seas. One thing was in his favor – he'd had no jacket on when he'd passed out and had been in only his socks – a pair of boots would have filled with water and sunk him in short order.

Well, he thought, here goes. I'd as soon drown as go where I'm headed.

He slipped his feet under the front thwart, took in as much air as his lungs could hold, then suddenly sat up, pushed at the same time with his arms and rolled over the side, all in one continuous motion. As he hit the water he heard Geezer yell, "Hey." Then he kicked himself deep, wiggling like a minnow. He stayed down as long as he could, trying to put distance between him and the boat, let himself surface, grabbed another chestful of air and sank again.

The splash of Dolf's hitting the water and Geezer's yell carried clearly across to the pursuing boat. Unwisely, Geezer followed his "Hey" with an oath and the loud remark, "That bastard Morgette rolled overboard."

It was all Knucks needed to throw him back into the oars. "Get with it, Grogan," he hissed, "and maybe I won't break yer neck when this is all over."

Diana had been in an agony of suspense ever since Dolf's telephone call. Now she was relieved only to realize quickly that Dolf might be tied hand and foot and would drown before they could reach him. They were at least a hundred yards away. She could dimly make out the other Whitehall boat across the water now. Despite her panic, or perhaps because of it, she luckily did exactly the right thing. She shouted, "Dolf, it's Diana. We're coming as fast as we can. If you can hear me, yell so we know which way to row."

She shouted just as he'd surfaced again to catch his breath. He was treading water, head back. He swiveled around to find out where Geezer's boat was before he risked yelling. Lucky for him that he did. It was bearing down directly at him not ten feet away, one of the occupants standing in the bow. He heard the one say, "Here he is," and the other yell, "Brain the bastard with an oar and let's get the hell out of here!"

Dolf let himself slip under, feeling an oar slap the water and graze his shoulder as he did. He kicked himself away as best he could, swallowing some water and desperately trying not to cough, knowing that if he did he'd take a noseful and start to drown.

Diana heard the shouted "Brain the bastard!" and, knowing that Dolf desperately needed help, risked turning loose both barrels, aiming above the other boat which was now only some fifty yards away. She was gratified to hear an anguished cry and the words, "My God, I've got it. Let's get out of here."

The next voice was Wyatt's. He yelled, "This is Wyatt Earp. Get off them oars! I've got a dead bead on you!"

"Okay!" Geezer yelled. "Don't shoot again. Harry's hit."

Dolf heard this exchange as he surfaced again, coughing and trying to keep his head above water as he did. Finally he was able to yell, "Over here, Wyatt!" He was tiring rapidly from his violent struggle, praying he could stay afloat till they negotiated the last several yards to him.

"Hang on, Dolf!" Wyatt yelled. "We're a-comin'!"

Dolf drew in a deep breath and floated awhile with his face in the water, bobbing just on the surface. Then he raised his head and gasped, "Make it quick."

He felt someone grab his hair and pull up his head. In a few seconds, several strong arms were hoisting him into the boat. He collapsed in the thwarts, gasping and coughing while Knucks pounded him on the back. Seeing that Dolf was all right, Wyatt turned his attention to the other boat. "Pull over here," he ordered, "and don't make any funny moves" — an order with which Geezer quickly complied.

Dolf rubbed his wrists briskly to restore the circulation. He glanced around, still breathless and a trifle groggy from the effects of the drug. He recalled hearing Diana yell, but her presence was so unexpected he more than half thought he'd been dreaming until she pressed near him and took over rubbing his wrists. "Oh, Dolf," she said, and threw her arms around his neck. "I thought you'd drown."

"That makes two of us," he replied.

They were interrupted by a bullhorn from across the water on the ship Geezer had been headed for.

"Ahoy. Need any help over there?"

Knucks, who'd been in the crimping business when the Barbary Coast was a pup, got an inspired idea. He yelled, "Not now. We're comin' alongside with a couple of recruits fer yuh. Okay?"

"Come ahead," the bullhorn responded. "We've been waitin'."

"Oh no," Grogan groaned. "No yuh don't."

"Oh yah," Knucks replied. "Yer gonna take a

cruise with yer pals over there."

With that, Grogan abruptly dived overboard. They could hear Knucks chuckling. He stepped over into Geezer's boat, grabbed him, and kicked him overboard after Grogan. Much to everyone's amazement, the wounded Harry leaped overboard after Geezer. Knucks shortly rejoined the others. "Damn it, Dolf," he complained, "I'm always missin' supper on account of you. Put 'er there, m'boy."

Dolf grasped his hand. "Supper's on me as soon as we get ashore."

"Py Gar, no. Supper's on me," Gabriel said.

"Who's that?" Dolf asked, getting up and peering at the big man. "Is that you, Gabe?"

" 's me, all right, you beeg fine sumbitch." Then he remembered Diana and said, aping the expression he'd so often heard, not realizing how funny he was being, "Oops, ma'am. Pardon my French."

Everyone laughed. Dolf accepted a huge bear hug from his old friend that rocked the boat perilously.

"Sit down, you two damn fools," Knucks ordered, "and let me row this thing ashore."

"Amen," Wyatt added. "I'll help."

They towed the other Whitehall boat behind them on its painter at Knuck's suggestion. "Harder rowin' this way, but this way those

184

three sweethearts'll probably have to swim over and jine their friends on board that ship. They'll like the cruise to China and the South Seas, or wherever it's goin'. Better yet, maybe it's a whaler — be gone only a couple o' years."

Dolf was wondering how Gabriel had happened to appear on the scene, since he'd only known him by his real name, Dufan. Then he began to speculate on the similarity between Dufan and DuMonde. He asked him, "Mornet wouldn't happen to be the sister you were planning to meet in San Francisco, would she, Gabe?"

"Yah" was all the big métis said, but its brevity was eloquent. Dolf suspected from this and his presence in this group that Gabriel had already discovered Mornet's undoubted part in having Dolf shanghaied. If he hadn't, Dolf didn't intend to mention it, instead planning to settle with her later himself. Gabriel cleared up his doubt about that with his next remark. "After she fix supper, I personal weel choke her neck plenty fo slippin' you the Meekie Feen. Dat damn sister. Bah!"

He sat the rest of the way to shore in disgusted silence. Knowing Gabriel as he did, Dolf wouldn't have been surprised at almost anything he might do. He recalled the trousers that he'd taken from two Canadian Mounted

Policemen to pay off an indignity. But he was sure he wouldn't strangle his little sister of whom he'd revealed so much pride whenever he'd talked of her in the past. On the other hand, what he did do would probably be rare and appropriate.

# Chapter 14

Dolf slept a lot later than usual, drained by his ordeal. Cow-country style, he'd provided Knucks half his bed. "We'll find you a place sometime," Dolf told him. He'd abandoned his friends' dinner party in his kitchen before the food even came, and had hit the hay; he hadn't even known when Knucks turned in. When he opened his eyes in the morning, Knucks was already up and out somewhere.

"Hey, Knucks," he yelled, "you still here?"

The other stuck his homely redhead in the door. "Couldn't stand yer snorin' anymore," he said. "Besides, yer pooch cold-nosed me and said he hadda go out."

Dolf grinned as Jim Too just then pushed past Knucks through the open door. "I'm glad he took to yuh right off."

Knucks snorted. "Right off, hell! It took me thirty minutes to convince him I oughta be allowed in bed last night. About ten pounds of supper scraps brought him around – so I'm warnin' yuh, he kin be bribed. By the way, I re-gnawed them bones myself this A.M. Don't yuh keep any grub in this joint?"

Dolf laughed. "Sorry I was too tired to tell yuh last night. Don't need any." He got up, led Knucks over to the dumbwaiter, and showed him how it worked.

"Cripes," Knucks said, "that's almost as good as the Army of the Potomac. We got to eat any-time some Reb wasn't watchin' his pigs and chickens. I think I'll buzz me up something."

"Why not wait a little while an' we'll go down-stairs. Can have it put on the table for us like the white folks do. It's always on the house, too, long as Will don't find us out an' can us."

"Might be a good idee. After what you got up that mine shaft last night, I don't know as I'd trust it," he said, indicating the dumb-waiter with his thumb.

"Don't worry," Dolf said over his shoulder, going into the bathroom, "after last night I don't think we have to worry about Mornet – that is, if Will don't can her."

"Never trust a skirt," Knucks yelled through the door, then, to emphasize his point, changed the inflection a little and added, "Nivver!"

Will phoned a short while later. "I'll see you

boys for breakfast shortly," he told Dolf. "We'll talk then — got a lot on my mind. Diana told me all about last night. I'm gonna lay into Mornet and chuck her out on her ear."

Dolf remained silent. "You still there?" Will asked. "I said I'm gonna can that dame."

"I wish you wouldn't," Dolf finally said.

"Why the hell not?"

"Dam'fino. I guess maybe because she's Gabe's sister. He saved my life once."

It was Will's turn for a reflective silence. Finally he said, "The hell yuh say? When?"

"Coupla years ago in Montana. And, by the way, did you know his name ain't DuMonde?"

"What the hell is it?"

"Dufan."

"I'll be go to hell. I should have guessed. Gabriel Dufan. As I recall, he whipped the Mounties and Canadian Army to a frazzle with a rag-tag mob. No wonder he's so damn hard." He paused, thinking that over. Finally he said, "You may be right. Maybe if I can her, I'll lose him, too."

"Maybe," Dolf said. "Most likely not. He's apt to think you oughta can her." Then he laughed. "But I don't. I kinda like her."

"Well, now don't that beat a hog flyin'? Are you sweet on her?"

"Nope. I just like her. She's got a lot of Gabe

in her. I think she'll be okay from now on."

"We'll talk about it," Will said. "I'll see you in about a half hour — don't wait on me if yer hungry."

The breakfast round table at the Latin Quarter was expanding remarkably. There were Will, Dolf, Gabriel, Knucks, and, a trifle later, Wyatt, who looked a little harried when he came in. Will eyed him critically. "What happened to you? You look almost as bad as Dolf ought to."

Wyatt flopped into a chair wearily. "Mrs. Earp happened to me. She finally got suspicious and decided I was out woman-chasing last night. I packed a suitcase and moved over to the Baldwin about three A.M. and finally got some sleep. Had a notion to call you, Dolf, and have you tell 'er what happened, but I knew you needed some sleep worse'n I did."

Dolf looked at him sympathetically, having seen Mrs. Earp at work before. "Want me to call her now?"

"Nope. Let 'er stew. She's probably over to her sister's place in Oakland by now, unloadin' her sorrows. She'll come around. Always does. About next week I'll get a Valentine and a box of candy from her sister's candy store."

Everyone laughed. Wyatt wasn't exactly a classic example of a case-hardened frontier lawman just then.

"Ah, women," Knucks sighed. "I was married once. Before the War. I got a letter from her the day of the Emancipation Proclamation sayin' she'd divorced me. I let out a whoop when I got the good news. The boys in the shanty naturally all wanted ta know what I thought I had to celebrate. I said, 'I'm free, boys.' I ain't nivver married agin since."

Even Wyatt joined the laugh over that. Dolf suspected there may have been as much as a slight grain of truth to the story, but not much more.

Mornet, who had been keeping out of sight, had to be summoned from the kitchen. Before sending for her, Will had talked over her disloyalty with Dolf and Gabriel. The latter had merely shrugged. He said, "I keek her ass agin if she need it. Do what you gotta, Will, I don' care."

Will decided to have a private talk with her in a booth away from the others. Compared to her usual radiant, vibrant self, Mornet was a sight, looking as though she'd spent a sleepless, conscience-stricken night. She couldn't bring herself to look Dolf's way. Finally Will returned to the others. "How about goin' over to talk to her, Dolf," he said. "I told her you wanted me to keep her here. She cried a little over that."

Dolf got up. "Keep yer guard up," Knucks muttered around a mouthful of biscuit.

Dolf seated himself across from Mornet, who had hunched herself together so she looked small and forlorn. Her head was down, eyes averted. Dolf spoke first. "It's okay, Mornet. We all make some pretty big mistakes."

She sobbed, still not looking at him. He wondered how much of it was an act. Knowing herself, so did she. She knew a man would normally be touched by her final submissive lifting of her tearful face. She regarded him with her tragic dark eyes, wet and huge. "Mornet ees so sorree," she sobbed. "And you are so — how you say — forgeeving of poor Mornet."

He reached across and took her hand. "It's okay, kid," he said. "Forget it. We'll take it from here."

She smiled tentatively. "I feex you a especial sopper, Morgette," she promised. "And I be yor slave." The thought brightened her up remarkably.

Oh oh, Dolf thought. This is where I came in.

He rose quickly and, squeezing her hand, said, "That won't be necessary, Mornet. Just be a good gal from now on." He rejoined the others hastily, leaving Mornet thinking furiously, her cap set for him just as firmly as ever.

192

She decided she was much happier, especially after his careless remark, "We'll take it from here."

"Well, now that that's settled I think we should all take a stroll over to the station house and have a leetle confab with Hanratty," Will suggested. "We can't prove a thing, since it's Mornet's word against his. Besides, her life wouldn't be worth a cent if he thought she was gonna testify. We couldn't sweat it outa Grogan an' his crew even if they were still around, which I'd bet they ain't. That leaves a heart-to-heart talk with the good captain to make him itch about where the suspenders cross just like the rest of us. How about it?"

As they walked toward the police station, Knucks asked Dolf, "How's that big ape, Champ Ryan?"

"Trainin' like mad, I hear."

"He's a good man," Knucks allowed. "You'll have yer hands full."

"Don't I know it."

"Don't worry, kid," Knucks added. "I got a few tricks in me bag I ain't showed yuh yet. Savin' 'em in case I hadda knock yuh on yer keester agin sometime. But this is a groundhog case. Besides, I might save one or two tricks anyhow. Main thing is git yez in shape."

"I'm comin' along," Dolf assured him. "If I

wasn't, I'd be feedin' the fish about now, I reckon. My wind and legs are in great shape."

"The two main things," Knucks stated. "You was born with shoulders like a buffalo. Yer old dad here'll git yez in shape."

Just then the cavalcade turned up the steps to the station house, Will and Gabriel in the lead.

"Where's his grace, captain Hanratty?" Will sarcastically asked the desk sergeant.

The sergeant eyed him benignly. "He ain't here."

"When'll he be in?" Will asked.

"In about two months, maybe."

Will looked surprised. They all were. "Where'd he go?"

"Took a coupla prisoners over to Sacramento and said he hadn't seen his sainted mother in twenty years and was goin' back to Boston for a visit."

Will exchanged a laden, disgusted look with the others. "I guess that takes care o' that." He looked back at the sergeant. "You're absolutely sure o' that?"

"Sure I'm sure. The captain ain't had a day off in ten years. He said he could use a rest. I kin believe it."

Will nodded, then turned and led the group back outside. "Well," he sighed, "at least we won't have any trouble with the bastard for a while — if he really is gone. Maybe he figured it'd be healthier to just lay low here."

"We'll know soon enough," Dolf said. "Any way to check up?"

"He's got a gal," Will stated. "Some of my boys know 'er. I'll check that angle. They're pretty thick. I don't think he'd leave town without her."

After the group split up, Dolf took Knucks and Gabe over to the Union Exchange to show them the gym. Wyatt decided to tag along. "I'll hang around the phone in Will's office in case any trouble comes up while yer workin' out, Dolf. It's a cinch I won't be missed around home, and I won't be goin' out to the track till this P.M."

Affairs settled down in the next few days to a routine. There was no trouble of the sort Hanratty had been causing around Will's joints on the coast. Dolf's days consisted of long sessions of road work, training exercises, and sparring at the gym. He managed to exercise Wowakan almost every day and saw Diana as often as they could manage without being too obvious. Will had provided Knucks an apartment at the Union Exchange on its famous third floor. When he discovered who his neighbors would be, he beamed. "Floozies. Scads of pretty gals. Well, waddya know about that? I'll hafta see that no harm befalls me pretty little neighbors."

Dolf snorted. "Father Geohagen himself! But don't let yourelf get too saintly — you might get snatched to glory before you get me trained fer that fight."

Knucks smirked. "Have no fears, lad. A man needs a little to talk about at confession."

Dolf would have bet he hadn't been in a church since he'd run away from home at about the age of twelve.

This small idyll of predictable routine came abruptly to an end. It started with an innocent-sounding invitation to lunch from Diana. He'd missed her usual appearance at his morning training bout. So had Knucks. He had been playfully sparring with her and actually teaching her a lot about self-defense. So had Jim Corbett.

"Hell," Knucks complained to Dolf. "I'll have to git on her about breakin' training. I was just getting her real good at Sabot. Woops. I wasn't supposed to tell you — she was plannin' to kick hell outa yuh by surprise in case you got fresh with her someday."

"She'll be in for the surprise. It was Sabot that I used on Champ. Surely your memory isn't slippin' in yer old age so that you forgot all you taught me about it?"

Knucks tapped his forehead. "The old man don't fergit anything," he said. "Except occasionally."

"Anyhow," Dolf told him, "I gotta go see our gal — her ma's throwin' a lunch for somebody they want me to meet — or most likely the other way around. I'm gittin' used to bein' a curiosity. Little old ladies pinch my muscles, then go off in the corner and whisper to each other about me not really lookin' like a mad-dog killer. I don't even get nervous anymore. Sometimes I go hide in the library and let them find me reading poetry. It really throws them." He sighed. "I'll be damn glad to get back to Alaska — if I ever find that SOB Twead. If he doesn't turn up pretty soon after I get this Ryan thing outa the way, I'm goin' anyhow, before the Yukon freezes up. I wanta make one more search in case my wife an' kid pulled through somehow. I'll tell yuh, Knucks, every once in a while I get the funniest feeling they ain't dead. I wake up at night after a dream and I can still see 'em there in the room."

Knucks clapped him on the shoulder. "I'm with you. I know how yuh feel. Maybe I'll throw in with yuh if you'll have me." There was no sign of kidding in Knucks's attitude.

197

"I'm serious," he said. "I've seen it all twice. I'd like to have a cabin a thousand miles from the nearest burg. I'd get me a squaw an' grow old an' die up there."

Dolf smiled, looking directly into the eyes of his old friend. "Yer on. You can probably batch in Doc Hennessey's old cabin. Maybe look after our diggin's."

"I'm your man," Knucks said fervently.

"Well, I gotta run and be cultured for a while," Dolf sighed. "See ya later." He was afraid, despite Diana's unconventionality, that he'd have to really be cultured if he married her. A hell of a lot more cultured than a fella wanted to. Especially one whose highest ambition was to run a nice, sheltered, well-watered cattle spread in some valley up in Idaho. He wondered how she'd take to the remote cabin he still owned on a homestead way up near the headwaters of Spruce Creek. He could see her being enchanted with it for about two days, then deciding they should go to breakfast at the Cliff House (five or six days away by train). He thought, Seems to me she's planning to show me Paris one of these days, too. I can hardly wait. At least they won't be able to give either of us Sabot lessons.

Diana herself met him at the door. "I've been waiting for you. I've got an old school girl friend I've got to show you off to. She's so refined she may swoon when she hears your name. So be ready to catch her. I invited her out for the rest of the summer, so she'll be here for your fight with Ryan. I haven't told her your name — just that you're famous — *and that you're mine.*"

She led him, somewhat breathlessly, into the library. A diminutive female with honey-blond hair had her back turned and was looking out the window as they entered.

"Victoria," Diana called, "I'd like you to meet Dolf Morgette — you've probably...." It was as far as she got. The woman had turned, and her face clearly registered surprised recognition before Diana had gotten his name out.

"Dolf," Victoria whispered in a small, cracked voice. Her arms involuntarily rose for a moment, and she took a tentative step toward him.

Diana's face was a study in conflicting reactions: surprise, shock, consternation, and finally, forced mirth. She tried to laugh, not quite successfully, since she hadn't quite fully assimilated the obvious. Then she found her voice. "Obviously you two are old acquaintances. Or is that the right word?"

Victoria blushed, but managed to smile. Dolf cursed himself for having lost his usual calm, especially when he observed Diana's stricken look.

Victoria supplied the word needed, though it was far from the fact. " 'Friends' is the right word," she said, still smiling. She advanced graciously and took both of Dolf's hands in hers. "We're from the same little town up north," she told Diana. "It's good to see you after all these years, Dolf. Did you forget how to write?" She stood on tiptoe and touched her lips lightly to his cheek, then drew back, hoping she didn't appear as breathless as she was. She had managed the casual remark about writing for Diana's sake, since she read plainly how this had struck her friend.

Dolf felt as breathless as she at again suddenly beholding in the flesh the radiant vision that had filled so many of his lonely dreams. She was lovelier than he remembered her that last night when he'd ridden away from her, as he then thought, forever. He had come to her house at night and seen her kissing Alby Gould in the arc of lamplight shining out the front door. As she had later explained, it had been an impulsive kiss given because of all they both owed Alby. Dolf had simply arrived at the worst possible time; in fact, he had come to propose to her, terribly aware that she was far above him.

Diana broke the tension. "I was going to say, 'I saw him first,' but I guess I can't even say that." She turned to Dolf. "I don't have to warn you about the spells this lady casts over men with her demure way, I can see. And having managed to say that much, let me add, let's go eat."

They were all relieved to have the tension broken, and laughed together. Victoria said to Dolf as they passed out of the room, "I'm dying to hear all you've been doing since you left Pinebluff."

For his part, Dolf was thinking, I'd have probably been a lot better off if we'd never met again.

But he was game, even eager, to see where this latest complication would lead in his disastrously scrambled affairs. He wasn't unhappy. The old spell had returned at the first sight of her — especially the calm, gray, long-lashed eyes, under graceful brows, perfectly accenting a poised face. Diana had used the right word when she'd said Victoria cast "spells" over men. But then, that had always been what enchantresses were about.

It wasn't a relaxed meal. Clemmy surmised what the situation might be as soon as she heard that Dolf and Victoria were old friends. She kept the conversation going in place of Diana, who was unusually quiet, thinking furiously.

What she was thinking, as she didn't hesitate

to admit to herself, was, Oh damn! I could kick myself. I only invited the Duchess [Victoria's nickname at school] to show off my big conquest. What rotten luck. Damn! Damn! Damn!

Dolf was being unusually attentive to Diana, recognizing that this had been a blow to her, but she felt resentful, as though he were trying to console a little girl who'd clumsily tripped trying to show off. Somehow, she feared, her life might not be the same after this day. She surprised herself by looking at Dolf and wondering how she'd feel about losing him. The prospect didn't seem as painful, at least just then, as she would have expected.

There would probably be someone else in time, she thought. But I'm not planning to lose him without a fight. Especially to the Duchess, of all women.

She felt better and began to join in the conversation. Clemmy smiled, knowing her daughter; she had correctly read what was going through Diana's head.

She'll survive in any case, Clemmy thought. But she needs someone like Dolf. A younger man could never keep her interested. And Dolf'll be the one she never forgets, no matter what happens.

Clemmy smiled wistfully. We'll see, she told herself.

# Chapter 15

Little Pete heard almost everything that went on in town practically as soon as it happened. He was one of the first to know that Hanratty had "pulled his freight" – and why. He was turning that over in his mind now.

He mused, Naturally, Alexander's crowd'll wonder if he's really gone or just underground. I know. They may not find out.

Therefore, he realized that anything under-handed he pulled off for his own advantage might still be laid at the captain's door. That set him to thinking in earnest. What could he do that might get Hanratty put out of his way, or at least strip him of his power? Something that would, at the same time, ingratiate him personally with Buckley.

For one thing, Pete decided he had to know more. This brought to mind the crooked detective Hanratty had mentioned – Pookay. Obviously the detective was made to order, a man after Pete's own heart – one who would do anything for money. Money Pete had in abundance.

If he could get Morgette out of the way before Hanratty blew back in town, Buckley would be more apt to see that he didn't need that Irish devil, Pete speculated. He knew that Buckley had gone through the roof when he'd heard that Hanratty had run out on him. Hanratty had obviously been scared out of his wits, afraid that Morgette would look him up and settle personally for the shanghaiing attempt.

It was no trick at all to have Pookay contacted and arrange to meet him privately. He preferred that the detective not know where he lived, so he met him at his restaurant, which was diplomatically (and perhaps facetiously) named the American Café. Little Pete was unobtrusively waiting for Pookay in the rear booth that he always reserved for business. As usual, he had his three white bodyguards and several of his Boo How Doy strategically seated at nearby tables and in the adjoining booths. A lot of people would have liked to see Little Pete put out of the way, especially rival tong leaders.

Pookay arrived right on time and was directed back to the rear booth, approaching suspiciously.

He correctly read the presence of several male parties strategically seated in the vicinity of the tong leader as bodyguards and made a point of avoiding sudden misleading moves. His trained nose suggested there might be a lot of money in any business with Little Pete. He was extremely curious to hear what proposition would be laid on the table, thinking, This crooked little character doesn't want to see the likes of me for some penny-ante deal.

Little Pete rose and greeted him, shaking hands like a white man and inviting, "Have a seat. Care to order something to eat while we're talking?"

This surprised Pookay. He'd learned of the czar of Chinatown but hadn't been around long enough to learn much about him. His surprise registered.

Pete laughed. "Maybe you thinkee Pete talkee like Chinee?"

Pookay didn't know how to take that, annoyed that his surprise over Pete's good English had been so obvious. Pete put him at ease. "I was raised in the U.S. since I was five. Now, how about some chow?" He handed Pookay a menu. It broke the tension.

The detective let out a relieved laugh. "Why not? I could stand something."

"How about a belt of something for an appetizer?"

That really pleased Pookay. He ordered straight whiskey and a big rare steak. He was beginning to think he would like Little Pete. That was exactly the way the Chinaman, a consummate psychologist, wanted it. He was a born confidence man with skills whetted by practice. After some general talk, he decided to come directly to the point (almost) in a way that Americans, actually the most devious of wheelers and dealers, had convinced themselves was the American way of doing business.

"Did you know your friend Hanratty has skipped town?" Pete asked.

This clearly elicited a surprised expression from Pookay. The thought flashed to his mind, How did this little bastard know about me and Hanratty? And Pookay hadn't known Hanratty had skipped either, so that added to his surprise.

Pete read his mind without much trouble on that one. "I know a lot of things," he said. "But so you don't think I'm a mind reader, Hanratty himself told me he'd known you for years."

Pete also read the thought that came to Pookay's mind over that, which was, I wonder what the hell else Hanratty told him about me?

Knowing he had Pookay off balance by now, Pete pressed his advantage. "No sense in beating around the bush. Hanratty told me Dolf Morgette had hired you for a little job." He let that sink in.

"So? Hanratty ain't no mind reader either. I told him about Morgette hirin' me," the detective shot back defensively. This was drifting into deep waters with unplumbed depths and making him uneasy. Nonetheless, he tried to appear deliberate in starting on his steak, which had just arrived. He didn't want to appear perturbed. Pete's inscrutable face and opaque hazel eyes made him nervous, with his seeming knack of reading his mind. He'd be damned if he'd ask why Hanratty had left town. He swallowed a mouthful and instead asked, "I expect this all fits into something you want done."

Pete nodded. "The same thing Hanratty wanted done."

"And what's that?"

"Don't you know?"

"I can guess. Get rid of Morgette – but it ain't gonna be easy. I know Morgette. He's not only tough, he's lucky. That counts for everything." His mind had started turning over the proposition of how someone would actually go about getting rid of Morgette, himself included. He'd risk anything for enough money, especially just then. No one who knew him would have suspected it, but he'd recently been thinking a lot about chucking the life he led and going back to a little farm in his home state, Kentucky. That would take a nest egg. He'd never been able to save a cent up till then. It was a combination of facts that made him vulnerable just now to greater risks than he was normally known to run. Besides, he thought, what Morgette don't know won't hurt me. Pookay was a great believer in the old double-cross, as long as he couldn't be found out.

"You want Morgette killed?" he asked.

Pete was silent for a moment, then said, "Maybe. That'd be risky. If we could just get him to blow, it'd be a lot better."

"Why do you want to get rid of him?"

Pete weighed the advantage of telling Pookay that. In fact, behind that question, he himself didn't know why Hanratty, through the Blind White Devil, was trying to run Will Alexander off the Barbary Coast. He wished he did. He merely assumed the more obvious reason — that Will was making big money they wanted for themselves. However, Pete was shrewd enough to allow for other, deeper motives, though he could hardly know the real one. In any case, it was obvious that Morgette stood in the way of the recent attempts to muscle Will Alexander off the coast. Not only stood in the way, but had done it so successfully as to run Hanratty out of town within a few weeks of taking a hand in the game. He could believe what Pookay had said about Dolf. He was not only pure poison, but he was indeed lucky. This line of reasoning gave him an idea how to answer Pookay's question.

"The main thing is to get Morgette out of Alexander's employ. Better not try to kill him if there's some other way. As you say, he's lucky as well as hard to handle." He savored the thought of how that had worked out for Hanratty. A deep hatred engulfed his mind whenever he thought how the captain had his way with Heavenly Flower, even with Pete around.

Pete's last remark had given Pookay an idea of how he might be able to milk some big dough from this situation. He hadn't let any grass grow under his feet in finding out why Diana had really wanted that flat. He'd staked it out himself to find out. He was satisfied he knew when he first saw Dolf let himself into the place with his own key while she was there. The second time he'd observed the two meeting there, he'd had not the slightest doubt about what was going on. This, added to what Little Pete had said, gave him the idea he had been grasping for. He'd already been trying to devise some scheme for milking blackmail from

Diana while being assured she didn't tell Dolf about it. Even using an intermediary, he was sure she'd have reasoned that only he would know enough to be behind a blackmail attempt. The idea that was forming in his mind would not only spike Morgette's guns, but might take Will out of the play as well. It would be risky. He'd have to disappear once he pulled it off. First he wanted more time to think it out fully before he presented a plan to Little Pete. He needed a way to be sure that the tong leader didn't simply use his information and muscle him out of the money. In such a case, Little Pete would make sure Pookay was no longer around to tell someone who had obviously stolen his secret. Leaving Little Pete in the dark would entail personal risk. His current plan would be to use one of Diana's visits to the flat as an opportunity to kidnap her. He'd have to pull that off personally. With her in his hands, Will Alexander could be forced to do almost anything — at the very least, discharge Morgette.

Pookay's long reflective silence prompted Little Pete to grin. "Do I hear wheels turning in your head?"

Pookay nodded. "I'll have to think about it, but maybe I know a way to get rid of Morgette for you without risking anybody's hide too much." He'd eyed the Chinaman speculatively, wondering it if was safe to push his luck. He thought, What the hell, push in your stack, Pookay, if you wanta smell that new-mown hay before you're tripping over your beard.

To Little Pete, who'd shown obvious interest, he said, "What'd it be worth to have Morgette just go away?"

Little Pete pretended to be thinking that over. He'd have paid a lot more but said, "Five grand — a thousand up front, the rest when you deliver."

Little Pete already knew how to make Morgette simply go away. But a sense of honor that few would have suspected in his warped nature prevented him from making the move. He could have thrown Twead to the wolves, either tipping Dolf off where to find him or scaring him out of town so Dolf would follow. The problem there might also be that Dolf would elect to stick it out with Will and follow later.

"Ten grand," Pookay upped the bid, pushing his luck some more."

"I'll let you know," Little Pete finally said, his eyes hooded. He wanted to talk to Buckley first. If he could get a promise from Buckley to get Hanratty out of his cue in return for disposing of Morgette, it would be worth ten G's. He didn't press Pookay for details; for one thing, he didn't want him to think he was that curious, and for another, the details didn't concern him if Pookay could actually deliver. Besides, he'd already decided to put a twenty-four-hour surveillance on the detective. He'd probably learn what Pookay was up to almost as soon as he pulled it off. Then he could decide whether to muscle in or pay up.

Little Pete's interview on this matter with the Blind White Devil was not very satisfactory to him. He naturally omitted mention of Pookay. All he elicited regarding the disposal of Hanratty was "We'll see. Get rid of Morgette first."

# Chapter 16

Diana Alexander planned to do a number of things about Victoria Wheat without bluntly suggesting, as she'd have preferred, that under the circumstances a lady ought to go home. She might have, but she suspected that Victoria would simply move out to the Palace or Baldwin, which would be worse for Diana than the existing situation. If she had read a letter Victoria once sent to Dolf, openly confessing her love for him, she'd have been even uneasier than she was. As things stood, she still had the consolation of a misconception that Victoria was self-possessed and perhaps a trifle cold. In that letter, Victoria had frankly stated to Dolf, "I must be a woman first." Diana would have recognized from this a woman not much different from herself, merely cooler on the surface.

These circumstances soon were destined to make Dolf's already complicated situation much more so. He was enough a gentleman that his relationship with Diana had frequently tweaked his conscience. He'd rationalized his behavior with the notion that he was going to make an honest woman of her someday, if he could. He wondered more and more often, however, if that would ever really happen. The actual circumstances pointed more toward her being obligated to make an honest man of him.

One thing that Diana definitely planned to do was avoid inviting Dolf to the Alexander house while Victoria was staying there. Another was to make sure Victoria never went to one of Dolf's sparring sessions. A third was to attempt to see Dolf as often as possible at her flat.

Diana was thinking of scalping her mother when she learned that Clemmy was planning a big evening party in honor of Victoria and had, without her knowledge, invited both Dolf and Gabriel Dufan. Clemmy had been enchanted to learn who Gabriel really was.

"That wild métis general who whipped the pants off the Canadians!" as she put it. She'd have been even more enchanted if she had known what he'd literally done to the pants of a couple of them who had particularly aroused his ire.

Gabriel wasn't the partying type — at least not that kind of party. His tastes ran more to undisguised wenching and heavy drinking. "Dem not Gabriel's kinda woman," he'd protested when Dolf had told him there'd at least be a lot of beautiful women at the affair.

"You can never tell," Dolf suggested slyly.

"What you mean, my friend?"

Dolf winked. "Wyatt's wife is a looker in more ways than one."

Gabriel eyed him for evidence that he was pulling his leg. "Ha," he snorted, "us Dufans not never rustle da neighbors' fillies."

"I see," Dolf said, tongue-in-cheek, "more or less a matter of honor, I suppose."

"Uh huh, more or less. Besides, my friend, you oughta go back look for Maggie stedda go to parties. Mebbe she still alive. I tink mebbe Gabriel go wit you. Will got lotsa dough — can get plenty fella like us. We go back." He was dead serious. He'd cried when he'd learned what had happened to Margaret and Henry. The big-hearted métis hadn't looked really happy since. He was brooding over his friend's unhappy fate.

"Soon," Dolf assured him. "But there's almost no chance they're still alive. Anyhow, I'm goin' back as soon as the job's done here. And you're dead right. Will can hire a dozen of our kind. I'm leavin' before freeze-up if I can find Twead by then. Don't even care about the fight with Ryan. Folks can say I ran out."

He heard himself saying it and could hardly believe his own ears. Morgettes weren't quitters or runners. He asked himself, What's ailing me? The answer wasn't long in coming. Women, he concluded. He'd regarded the prospect of marrying a society woman, especially one almost twenty years younger, with a great deal of uncertainty, at least – perhaps panic was more the case. As he learned more of her ways, he suspected that someday, perhaps even soon, an older man wouldn't be able to keep pace with Diana's youthful enthusiasms, particularly an older man with whom she really had only one mutual interest. Passion cools with time. He was certain he didn't want another tragic, broken marriage. In the back of his mind, another voice prodded him: How much of this big, noble change of heart was due to Victoria Wheat being there now? He frankly admitted to himself that he didn't know. In any case, there were exactly the same objections regarding marriage to Victoria. I wonder if she'd still have me? was a thought he could hardly avoid. The whole perplexing situation made a return to Alaska seem like an attractive escape. And he had such a plausible and compelling excuse for doing that. He planned to strongly push the effort to turn up Twead so he could leave with a clear conscience.

When Gabriel learned that Twead had hired Harvey Parrent's murder, he had exploded, "That Cochan sumbitch! If I get my hands on ees neck, I wring it like a chicken." Dolf and Harvey had met Gabriel on the same day back in Montana. He had driven them out to show them available homestead land. Gradually they'd all become close friends.

The fleeting notion occurred to Dolf of persuading Gabriel to stay and seek Twead while he himself returned north. If Gabriel was serious about Alaska, he could follow later.

What the hell's wrong with me? Dolf exploded inwardly, dissatisfied with that sort of thought. Us Morgettes always killed our own beef. I must be gettin' soft. When a man does that, he's ridin' for his last fall. That had always been an article of faith with him during his outcast years. Maybe my time is coming, he thought. So be it.

"I guess we'd better get our trottin' harness on, Gabe, if we're gonna shine at Clemmy's party," he said.

There were a lot of Will's old Virginia City friends at any party Clemmy gave. When Dolf and Gabe arrived in a hack, they could hear the party going full blast from down the street.

"Sounds like Fort Belton on Saturday night," Dolf observed.

"Yah," Gabe agreed. He looked thoroughly uncomfortable, shoehorned into evening clothes that Will had provided.

Clemmy obviously had plans to lionize her favorite guerrilla general, a fact mercifully unknown to Gabe, or he'd have fled to the hills. She grabbed him at the door to steer him off on a round of introductions.

"Hello, Dolf," she said briefly. "I hope you don't mind my stealing your friend and leaving you on your own. You know most of these people by now."

Gabriel gave him a drowning, don't-desert-me-now look, to which Dolf responded with a mischievous grin and merely waved his fingers good-bye at him. About then Diana descended on Dolf, intent on keeping him under a watchful eye, if not actually on her arm, all evening.

"Hi," she greeted him. "I missed you." She hadn't seen him since his morning training session — almost eight hours. He grinned down at her affectionately.

"I ain't exactly been out of town," he protested, still grinning a little and suspecting what might be at the root of this sudden unusual ardor.

"I miss you when you're out of sight," she said.

He swept his eyes briefly around the big ball-room when they entered, looking for the possible location of the root of Diana's unusual warmth. Victoria was not in sight, but he'd bet that a tight knot of men over in a far corner denoted her location — she'd be surrounded by them. Diana steered him to the liquor, although she knew he drank very little. It was as far away from Victoria as she could get him. He obligingly followed her into an unobtrusive corner behind a fluted column and turned his back on the room, juggling a glass of champagne punch for appearances; he didn't care much for its taste. Normally Diana would have attracted several men like a magnet, a fact that always pleased her immensely. Tonight he had her to himself; Wyatt Earp hadn't even showed up. He noticed Diana's irritated glance turned toward the cause of her desertion tonight. A faint frown captured her face, but she quickly erased it. Eventually Ambrose Bierce joined them, bowing to Diana formally, then shaking Dolf's hand.

To Dolf he said, "You're looking trim. The whole town's waiting for the big match to come off next week."

"I'll be glad when the whole fuss is over," Dolf said. He watched Diana obliquely as he very deliberately added, "I'd like to get back to Alaska before freeze-up and make one last search

219

for my wife, just in case."

Surprise, then dismay, crossed Diana's face before she caught herself. Bierce, who was a very perceptive individual, suspected how it was between Dolf and Diana. He'd quickly surveyed Diana's face and read her expressions just as Dolf had. Dolf suspected Bierce's reaction amounted to a shrewd surmise. Quickly covering her consternation, Diana said lightly, "I hoped we'd have you till next spring, Dolf."

Further talk along that line was forestalled by someone approaching from behind and lightly touching his arm. "I've been watching for you to arrive, but you sneaked in," Victoria Wheat reproved him, joining the group.

No reaction to her arrival was readable in Diana's expression, but Dolf could imagine what it was. Bierce, whose intuitions were almost uncanny when it came to people's thoughts, was watching this byplay between the other three closely, sensing some undercurrent.

"Shame on you, Diana," Victoria chided her with mock seriousness. "You've been keeping Dolf hidden all week. After all, we are old friends. Besides," she added calculatedly, "I used to have a schoolgirl crush on him when he was the handsomest deputy sheriff in Idaho."

Bierce eyed Victoria appreciatively. He admired her cool injection of herself into a situation from which he suspected, rightly, that she was being deliberately excluded by Diana. And he gave Diana at only twenty, equally high marks for her outwardly calm acceptance of what was happening. He chuckled inside. His next remark to Diana forestalled the social shooting match that might have ensued. "Young lady, I can appreciate why you're keeping susceptible old gallants like me away from your lovely friend here, but I must point out that we haven't been introduced."

This definitely defused the tense situation. Diana performed the introduction with a small laugh. "Mr. Bierce is a famous writer," she added.

"Not true, my dear Miss Wheat. I'm actually the first, and perhaps the last, of the six-shooter essayists." Seeing Victoria's slightly puzzled look, he explained. "I do what's known as calling 'em like ah see 'em. As a result, I'm reputed to carry two six-shooters to back up my viewpoint."

Victoria laughed appreciatively. "Do you?" she asked.

"Of course," he admitted. Then they all laughed. "I'm also reputed to be nuts," he added. When no one said anything, he remarked, "I had hoped that a young lady as refreshingly direct as you would also ask to that, 'Are you?' To this I answer for you, in case you were thinking of asking that, 'Yes, somewhat,' especially in the full of the moon."

"Oh dear," Victoria said. "As I recall, we're having a full moon now."

"Yes indeed," Bierce said. "And if you'll all excuse me, I'm going out into the grounds and bay at it."

He bowed to the ladies, nodded to Dolf, and departed across the room.

"What a fascinating man," Victoria observed. "If he's crazy, it's like a fox, I'd guess."

"Yes," Dolf said.

The first of Victoria's coterie of admirers to approach her as she stood with Dolf was Wyatt Earp. He was still a happy temporary bachelor. He looked more carefree than Dolf had ever seen him.

"Hello, Wyatt," Dolf greeted him.

"Evenin', Dolf, Diana," he murmured, but his eyes were all for Victoria, a fact that irritated Diana at once, since he'd been pursuing her for months. "Your glass is empty, Miss Victoria," Wyatt said, "may I get you another champagne punch?"

She smiled at him in her poised manner. "Why, yes, I'd like that." He was off like a dog after a covey of quail, forgetting to ask Diana, who had no drink, if she'd like something.

Before long Dolf was crowded by the swains who had followed Victoria across the room, a crew from eighteen to eighty, some tolerably sober, others gallantly tipsy, but all there in Victoria's orbit. She still clung to Dolf's arm. In exasperation, Diana glued herself to the other one.

Bierce strolled past again a little later and winked knowingly at Dolf over the tops of several heads. "A terrible fate, Dolf," he called, loudly enough to make himself heard. He waved and departed to join the crowd of women congregated around Gabriel and Clemmy. Dolf could see his friend over the intervening heads. He seemed to be rapidly adapting to this crowd and enjoying himself. Probably drunk by now, Dolf thought. I wish I was.

A plan was forming in Diana's mind to make it clear to Victoria just how serious things were between her and Dolf. She'd been particularly annoyed to hear him invite Victoria to one of his training sessions. The call to dinner finally unglued Victoria from Dolf's arm. Diana had seen to it in advance that she herself was next to Dolf and that Victoria would sit far away. She thought she knew how to chill any notion Dolf might have to see Victoria alone sometime. She whispered to him, "I'll be waiting tomorrow afternoon."

Where women were concerned, Dolf was still a trifle naive for his age, but he suspected what might have prompted the suggestion at that moment. A perverse notion grasped him, impelled by his dry sense of humor. He looked at her very seriously and replied in a low voice, "Normally I'd be there with bells on, but Knucks says nix till after the fight. Part of training."

He had a hard time to avoid grinning at the look Diana gave him. His needling remark redoubled her plan to put Victoria in her place. She wondered, Is he planning to meet *her* tomorrow?

For her part, Victoria could see how things were without any further broad hints from Diana. She had no plans to try to go out of her way to interest Dolf anew, she assured herself. Or did she? She was too used to being absolutely honest with herself. The old warmth had returned when she'd first seen him again. I've never even kissed him, she thought. Talk about your schoolgirl crush. What is it about him? Every woman I've ever seen around him feels it.

Late that night, after the party had broken up, Victoria lay awake in bed a long while, thinking. She recalled Dolf as he'd looked, gaunt and pale after he'd been released from prison. Her father had employed him as a partner since he'd studied law during those lost five years. But Mark Wheat had actually wanted Dolf more as a bodyguard.

She hadn't seen Dolf in years before the night they'd carried him upstairs in the Wheat house his first night home — he'd almost been killed by smoke inhalation after rescuing several people from a fire at the jail. Doc Hennessey had drafted her as Dolf's nurse. She remembered that they hadn't been sure if he might not have scorched his lungs and would die. He'd finally opened his eyes and looked at her, perplexed, trying to figure out where he was. He'd looked so wildly at her that she'd thought he must be dying. Her feeling of panic then returned to her now as she relived the moment. She had been about to run for help when he'd suddenly smiled.

To conceal her moment of panic and break the tension, since she sensed his confusion and the reason for it, she had said, "I'm Victoria Wheat."

"I know," he'd said. "I always thought you'd grow up to be a rare beauty." He'd paused for a moment while she started to blush, then added, "And you did."

Then he'd flopped back on the pillow and fallen asleep at once. She smiled, remembering how relieved she'd been to know he wouldn't die.

She herself went to sleep remembering that appealing, boyish smile, even though he'd otherwise looked prematurely old. Her last thought was, If I still want him, I can have him.

# Chapter 17

Wyatt Earp had been coming down to Will Alexander's gym and refereeing formal matches between Dolf and his sparring partners. The best of them, next to Knucks, was turning out to be Jim Corbett. He was in A-number-one condition, learned fast, had a fighting heart and the speed and coordination of an angel.

"Watch that young feller," Knucks told Dolf. "In a few years he'll clean all our plows in the ring."

"I can believe that," Dolf agreed. "He's a handful right now."

This was the session to which Dolf had invited Victoria. Naturally, Diana was chaperoning her — in the guise of accompanying her, of course. Victoria gave the action her rapt attention. She'd never seen anything like it. Her eyes were shining over watching Dolf easily handle these big, violent fighters, ending up hardly breathing hard. She went to him as soon as the last round was over.

"Are you really trying to knock each other down?" she asked Dolf naively.

He had to laugh. "You bet. You can't pull punches and get in shape for a serious bout. They aren't only trying to knock me down but out cold."

"I notice it wasn't you who got knocked down."

"Good legs," he told her. "I'm always fading away when they hit me. Knucks calls it staying on yer hoss. It isn't the way anyone I ever saw boxed before he came along. If they do hit you, it doesn't have the mule kick that knocks a man down. My two old-timers there think it's a sissy way to box, but it's not against the new rules — the Marquis of Queensbury rules. On the other hand, Corbett took to it like a duck to water."

He sat on the bench next to Victoria, swabbing his sweaty face with a towel. He was amused to see Diana making a big play to engage both Wyatt and Jim Corbett in an animated conversation, covertly watching to see if Dolf noticed. He pretended not to, hearing her laugh a little too loudly a couple of times.

"That was my last training session," he told Victoria. "The bout is night after tomorrow. How about taking you and Diana for lunch at the Latin Quarter to celebrate my being allowed to be lazy for a couple of days? Got some of the best chuck in town."

"Yes – and soon, I hope. I'm starved. I must have worked up an appetite watching you do the work."

"Soon as I take a shower and get dressed. Tell Diana."

"Should *I* tell her?" she asked uncertainly, knowing he'd understand her meaning.

He grinned. "Why not? If she doesn't want to come, we'll go without her."

Diana had been formulating a plan that necessitated her getting away for a few hours. She'd ordered what amounted to a couple of stage props and had to pick them up. As a result, rather than being miffed over Dolf's inclusion of Victoria in a luncheon invitation, she welcomed the excuse to get away.

"I've got to run some important errands for Papa," she lied to Victoria. "Dolf will understand. I may join you for dessert if I get done in time." She smiled a trifle too sweetly as she added, "Promise me he'll be safe with you alone."

"Promise," Victoria replied, then added as an afterthought, "But how about me? I've never been alone with Dolf – will I be safe with him?"

Diana eyed her coolly. "I don't know him all that well, either," she lied, savoring the fact that she'd soon have her chance to make clear just how well she *did* know him. "But if you survive, I have a secret I want to show you this afternoon. I'll meet you at the Latin Quarter or, if I'm late, at the house."

"I love secrets," Victoria said.

When Dolf rejoined Victoria, the rest had already left. "You're stuck with me by myself, I guess," she said.

"I guess I'll be able to bear up," he said. "In fact, I love it."

She explained Diana's absence. Dolf wondered how much truth there was in her excuse. He wouldn't have been surprised if she had gone to lunch with Wyatt or Jim Corbett, just to spite him. Nor, in the latter case, if she had issued the invitation herself and would pay the bill. He knew she was trying to make him jealous. If she went to lunch elsewhere, he expected she'd contrive for him to hear where she'd been and with whom. He also knew she liked men — lots of them. If his experience was a fair gauge, he knew she had eyes for *one* man for only about a month, or two at the most. He was not displeased. It would make what he was coming to realize he had to do, sooner or later, all the easier for him when the time came.

As their eyes adjusted to the subdued light of the Latin Quarter, Victoria exclaimed, "I love this décor!"

Dolf wasn't exactly sure what a décor was, but suspected. He said, "I like it here. I live upstairs."

She hadn't known that. She turned the idea over in her mind of asking to see his quarters. She wondered if he'd consider such a suggestion forward and unladylike. An unaccustomed internal conversation occurred behind her usual cool facade. Ladylike, be damned! she told herself. Outwardly she smiled at him disarmingly. "Are you going to invite me into your parlor?"

He wasn't sure where such a question led, especially from a woman like her, but he'd learned a lot from Diana. If she hadn't led, he'd have hesitated even to hold her hand. Without undue hesitation, he shot back, "Why not?" He couldn't avoid entertaining the notion that it would be a delicious joke on Diana if she came to join them belatedly and discovered they were upstairs. He had allowed her upstairs only that one time, and then only to show her the place. He realized the particular need in her case, as Will's daughter, to preserve proper appearances.

Mornet DuMonde was a study in perplexity when she saw Dolf with a strange woman, and a beauty at that, particularly when Diana failed to show up on time and Dolf led Victoria through the kitchen, obviously headed up to his apartment. Dolf relished Mornet's probable consternation, denoted by a heavily laden silence. He was thankful she held her tongue. She appeared to have learned her lesson. He hadn't told Victoria of Mornet's part in the attempt to shanghai him, and judging from Victoria's lack of interest in Mornet, he concluded that no one else had either.

"How lovely!" Victoria exclaimed over the richly carpeted stairwell with its varicolored illumination from the stained-glass windows.

"You ain't seen nuthin' yet, ma'am," Dolf assured her, being deliberately droll. He unlocked the upstairs door, then pushed it open, motioning her in ahead of him.

He was happy to observe the pleased expression that viewing the sumptuous interior for the first time brought to her face. She turned and faced him, gently placing her hands on his lapels.

"I'm so happy you're doing so well here," she said. But it was obvious that wasn't the meaning of her gesture. Invitation was plain in her eyes. There was no uncertainty mirrored there. He was tantalized by the subtle fragrance of her perfume. Still he hesitated. She laughed lightly, pressing against him. "We've never even kissed," she whispered. "Go ahead, I won't break."

Gently he placed his fingers on her soft shoulders, then pretended to check her durability with his fingers, regarding her mirthfully for a moment. "No, I don't reckon you'll break," he concluded. He had no idea where this was leading — she had a definite idea. The kiss was very gentle at first. She pressed herself to him and broke the dam of his long-pent-up hunger for this to happen someday. He was surprised to discover that she was not a novice at kissing, as he had naively expected she would be. She opened her eyes. They were almost black with sudden passion. He kissed her more roughly. When they relaxed momentarily, she drew back and inhaled deeply, shaking her head in confusion over her sudden overwhelming response to being held and kissed by him.

"I've waited a long time for this, Dolf." She didn't want to break the spell, but she had to know something before she went further. "I sent you a letter from Pinebluff after you left — did you get it?"

He nodded. "And tried to answer it about a dozen times. You know I got married?"

"Yes. And about what happened in Alaska. I'm so sorry, Dolf." She paused, watching him.

"But I'd be a liar if I said anything has changed. I still love you. It's silly. We hardly know each other, but I know I'll always love you."

He drew her close again. She looked up at him, her face warm and flushed. "I'm not the angel you may think I am." She paused, then said breathlessly, "I want you."

Her meaning was crystal clear. It could be read in her eyes. His surprise was obvious. "Here? Now?" he asked. Her face was even more flushed, but she said unhesitatingly, "Anywhere. Anytime. Why did you think I asked you to come up here? I may never see you alone again."

He didn't know what to say, if anything. He thought of telling her about Diana.

She read his mind. "I'm not worried about Diana, or what she'll think. She's a big girl now, but still she's almost a child. I'm not. She expects me to meet her at the house if we're not downstairs when she stops by. She would never suspect me, of all people, of coming up here. Or won't till I'm back late. Wondering why will do her good."

He laughed. "That's so." The idea appealed to him. He was getting to know Diana a lot better — and believe her a lot less. In fact, he had his suspicions about her willing absence at lunch, though they were wrong in this case.

He unhesitatingly drew Victoria into his arms again. Her soft, warm lips met his eagerly.

It was midafternoon when Victoria finally reached the Alexander place. She dropped off the cable car a block away and walked, arriving somewhat breathlessly. She composed herself before she entered. She half-expected Diana to meet her at the door. She didn't, but wasn't long in putting in an appearance.

"Where in the world have you been?" she asked suspiciously.

"Where in the world have *you* been? We waited ever so long for you."

"You weren't there when I ducked in. I expected you here by the time I got home."

"I just had to see Dolf's apartment. We thought you'd come up looking for us. When you didn't, I decided to walk home, it's so nice out — and I'm sorry you expected me sooner — I didn't know; I guess I rubbered in all the store windows on the way."

Diana's look clearly said she didn't believe a word of it.

Victoria coolly turned her back, casually removing her gloves, then her hat, at the hall mirror. "It's true," she said calmly. "Doesn't Dolf have a lovely place? I wouldn't go up like that with every man — or I should say, any man — but Dolf is always a gentleman. Don't you think so?" she asked brightly, turning to smile at Diana. Suspicious as she was, Diana simply couldn't bring herself to believe the obvious about the Duchess, of all people.

Diana became satisfied her suspicions had been foolish. She looked closely at her friend, nonetheless, for any evidence of dissimulation. Finally she laughed. "Victoria, you're so innocent. And proper. Maybe that's why I like you so much. I'm just the opposite."

Victoria feigned surprised interest. "Is it confession time? What does that mean? I suppose you're not innocent? You're almost still a child." She played the role of concerned friend with consummate skill.

Diana assumed a conspiratorial air. "That's part of the secret I was going to let you in on. Put your hat and gloves back on. We're going gadding. Maybe you won't think I'm such a child...or—" She had almost said, "or that Dolf is such a gentleman," but thought better of it.

Victoria could imagine what she had been about to say.

They took the cable car downtown, then hailed a hack. Inside Victoria asked, "May I inquire where you're taking me?"

"You may, but I won't tell. It's only a short ways now."

Diana had become less cautious in going to the flat since no one seemed to pay much attention to her there. She always spoke to the neighbors on the few occasions she'd seen them, but neither she nor they had made an attempt at any greater familiarity. She took the hack directly to the front now, rather than walking the last block as she had at first when she had felt self-conscious. She had taken the precaution of actually moving in artist's supplies and setting up a studio for appearances. She actually did paint remarkably well. She frequently dawdled at it while she waited for Dolf. This provided a means to conceal from Victoria her true purpose in bringing her there. Victoria could naturally draw her own conclusions. Diana had carefully arranged things to assure what those conclusions would be.

"I've got a hideout of my own," she announced after she'd paid off the hack driver. "Follow me. Clemmy and Papa think a poor little rich girl shouldn't have amibitions to be an artist, so I got my own studio. They don't know about it."

She led the way up the three flights of stairs. The cigar smoke was noticeable as soon as they were inside. Diana thought, Dolf must be here now.

That puzzled her because he'd never come

unannounced. But all the same it pleased her, since the added thought occurred, How perfect. I can hardly wait to see Victoria's face — and his.

She almost laughed.

Only it wasn't Dolf who stepped out of the bedroom hallway. It was a masked man with a six-shooter pointed at them.

"Don't scream or try to run, ladies, and nobody will get hurt," Pookay's muffled voice ordered from behind his mask. He didn't sound any too steady, and he wasn't. He'd heard Diana talking to someone as she'd come up the stairs and had naturally assumed it was Dolf. It had given him a bad moment. He'd almost passed out from relief when he heard another female voice answer her. He wasn't too happy that she wasn't alone, but two females were a small problem compared to Dolf.

Just that morning Little Pete had given Pookay the green light to dispose of Dolf by whatever means he had in mind, in return for ten grand. He didn't even bother to inquire into the details of Pookay's plan, and therefore didn't know he was going to try to kidnap Diana, but he would in due time, since he'd had Pookay shadowed for days.

In Pookay's eyes, Diana was only an inconsequential young girl — moreover, a society dame at that — and so her sudden attack took him entirely off guard. As Knucks had taught her, she caught Pookay with a perfectly aimed kick to precisely the right location to put a man out of business in a hurry. He doubled up, groaning, and caught a second kick to the side of his head that dropped him to the floor unconscious. Diana picked up the six-shooter from where he'd dropped it. He hadn't even taken the precaution of cocking it, since he'd expected an easy time of it dealing with "only" women.

Victoria had looked surprised at her first sight of Pookay, but wasn't necessarily afraid. She'd assumed he was probably a burglar they'd caught in the act, and that he would be happy simply to get away. However, she was astounded at Diana's almost instantaneous reaction.

Diana laughed shakily. "Us Alexanders are a tough crew," she said with a bravado she didn't feel. Her lightning reaction had surprised even her. "I don't have a telephone," she said, practically. "We'll tie him up before he comes to, and then one of us can go call for help." She had presence of mind enough to put as much of her original plan into effect as possible. She made sure that Victoria saw the *Dolf* carved in the belt she brought out to help truss up Pookay. She'd planned to have it in plain sight when she showed Victoria the bedroom, along with two silver brushes on the dresser monogrammed with M's. Purchasing them and putting them in the apartment was what had occupied her lunch hour.

Diana concealed her amazement when they pulled the handkerchief mask from Pookay's face. She didn't know what to make of his being there, but intended to think it over before she told Victoria who he was. All she said was "Victoria, you'd better go find a telephone and call someone. Try to get Dolf. He knows where this place is," she added significantly. "If we call the police, it could get into the papers, and I don't want Clemmy and Papa to know."

Victoria wasn't thinking too clearly, but that made sense to her. She dutifully did as Diana suggested. She was relieved to reach Dolf himself at the number Diana had given her. The words tumbled out in a rush, telling him only roughly what had happened.

"I'll be right over," he said, slamming the phone down.

He arrived at a gallop on Wowakan. Victoria met him outside, looking frightened. She yelled to him, "When I got back, they were both gone; it looks like she put up a fight. Things are knocked over."

He took the steps two at a time. The door

was still standing open. Inside there was plenty of evidence that Diana hadn't gone peaceably along with whoever had abducted her.

Dolf asked Victoria, "Is there any chance that guy could have got loose?"

"I don't think so."

He went downstairs to each of the apartments below to inquire whether the occupants had seen or heard anything. No one answered on the second floor. The woman home on the first hadn't heard or seen a thing. She regarded Dolf suspiciously, almost afraid to talk, although she'd seen him before. She quickly shut the door, looking puzzled, after briefly telling him nothing helpful.

He rejoined Victoria, who had wandered around the third-floor apartment and had inadvertently got Diana's other message, the monogrammed brushes. She hadn't been shocked. In fact, she was pleased to discover confirmation of what she herself had recently learned — that Dolf wasn't as backward with women as he appeared on the surface.

Dolf said, "That fellow must have had someone with him. Whoever it was may even have been hidden right here when you left. Did you get a good look at the one you tied up?"

"I'd never seen him before, but I'd know him if I ever saw him again."

Dolf was recalling Diana's remark — made in jest, he thought — about leading a secret life. He wondered if that might not have been the joke he took it for.

"We can't do any more good here." He was wondering how to break the news to Will; he'd have to find out about this apartment now, and would probably suspect the truth. "I've got to tell Will and call the police," he told Victoria.

She regarded him with surprise. Reluctantly she reminded him, "Aren't you going to get your things out of here before you do?"

He registered his surprise. "I don't have any things in here."

Silently she left and returned with the silver brushes.

"They aren't mine," he told her truthfully. But he surmised what they had been doing there. Victoria looked dubious. "It's true," he assured her. "Maybe she was going to give them to me."

She smiled wickedly at him. "What I'm learning about you all in one day," she said, registering her obvious disbelief.

"That goes two ways," he retorted. But they both realized their joking covered their deep concern for the missing Diana.

When Dolf called the police after conferring

with Will by telephone, he learned that Captain Hanratty had returned, if he'd ever really left. He wondered if the Captain himself might have had a hand in Diana's abduction.

"I'll damn well find out," he swore. "And a couple of other things from that skinny, long-nosed bastard."

He was deeply concerned for Diana's safety. Whatever his true feelings for her may have been, and he wasn't at all sure about them, he was extremely fond of her, even at her worst.

# Chapter 18

Will Alexander got the ransom note the night Diana disappeared. There were two conditions: *Make sure Morgette leaves town, and be sure Champ Ryan wins their bout before he leaves.* Will got in touch with Dolf on the phone at once.

"It don't take a genius to figure who's got her," Dolf guessed. "Whoever wants to run you off the coast, which spells Hanratty and Co. They must've seen a good chance to clean up some extra money at the same time, since I'm about a two-to-one favorite after kicking hell out of Ryan once before."

"Maybe," Will said. "But kidnappin' a gal ain't Hanratty's style, whatever else you say about him."

Dolf was doubtful. He was surprised at the depth of feeling he'd discovered in himself for his lovely young companion of the past few

244

weeks, now that he might never see her alive again. To Will, he said, "All the same, you say the word and I'll take Wyatt and Gabe and Knucks over and drag the Irish bastard out of his own station house and choke it out of him, if he knows anything."

"Don't," Will cautioned. "Hanratty was over here a while ago, really worried, and told me he didn't have a damn thing to do with it — and said he'd move heaven and earth to find the girl for me. He wasn't lying, I don't think. Even you'd have believed him if you'd seen the way he looked. Heaven help me if I'm wrong, but I believe the man."

"So what do we do?"

"Sit tight." He hesitated a long while. He finally said, "Do what you have to about the fight, Dolf."

"Hell, Will, I'm gonna do what they want and take a dive. I thought you'd know that."

There was a near sob in the older man's voice as he said, "Thanks, Dolf. I'll tell Clemmy that. She was almost out of her mind, but even at that she didn't want you to throw the fight unless you thought you ought to." He hung up.

On the following day, the marquee of the Union Exchange carried the illuminated sign *O.K.* Passersby may have wondered what this announced. It was Will's acceptance of the kidnappers' demands, displayed as they'd specified in their note. The fight was one day away. Diana's disappearance had been kept out of the papers with Hanratty's cooperation.

"It'd be bad enough losin' to that big Irish stiff fair 'n square," Knucks lamented. "This way, if the word gets out ya took a dive, it'll dog ya the rest o' yer life."

"I don't give a damn," Dolf replied. "I'll make it look good though. Do you think the Champ might be in on it?"

"Hell, no. I know the big stiff like a brother," Knucks said quickly. "He ain't exactly honest, except about some things. This'd be one of 'em. He has to beat you fair 'n square in a case like this. If I'da thought he knew something, I'da been over to see him before now."

The fight crowd almost all showed up for dinner at the Union Exchange. By ring time they were mostly pretty well oiled and yelling for action. Wyatt, as referee, got into the ring in evening clothes, like the born showman he was, casually shucked his coat and handed it to Knucks at ringside, along with a six-shooter he'd had in his back pocket. The crowd loved it, roaring their approval.

Champ came down the aisle to the ring first, thirty pounds lighter than the day Dolf had laid him out, looking fit and ten years younger from a couple of months off booze and high living. His backers cheered and yelled encouragement to him.

Dolf came shortly, narrow-waisted and broad-shouldered with massive arms — nonetheless many pounds lighter than Ryan — looking to neither side as he came rapidly down the aisle. He was preoccupied with his thoughts of Diana and what he had to go through for her sake. He harbored no resentment, not even deep inside. Life handed it out, people did what they had to. He knew what he had to do. But first I'll make the Champ sweat, he consoled himself grimly.

At the sound of the first-round bell, he drifted out like a fast-moving shadow, rocking Ryan with a series of left jabs, then staggering him with a right cross. (He was pacing himself to go the limit, however, knowing that this was to be one of the country's first fights limited to a specified number of rounds — fifteen in this case.) Champ had expected the smaller man to be cautious and feel him out. This attack took him off guard. He bellowed, stung by the flurry of punches, and missed with a wild retaliatory roundhouse counterpunch that Dolf easily ducked under, grinning at the Champ. Champ next charged with his own flurry of punches, looking stunned when they all landed in thin air. Dolf slipped away back-ward faster than Ryan could follow coming forward. He was used to the old rules, under which the fighters stood toe to toe at the scratch line and slugged away at each other. At the ropes, Dolf side-stepped the pursuing Champ like lightning and dropped Ryan with a single murderous chop to the side of his head — not hard enough to put him out, but enough to show him who was boss. He was back up be-fore Wyatt started a count. Ryan's ear was fiery red where the cutting blow had landed. He looked around for Dolf like a bear that had just been stung by a wasp.

As they closed again, he growled, "Stop bein' a Fancy Dan. Stand up an' fight."

Dolf merely grinned, dancing in and rocking him with another series of short jabs, almost exactly repeating the previous sequence. Ryan hadn't learned from the last exchange and blun-dered after Dolf to the ropes, being decked again just as before, in almost the same spot in the ring. Again Dolf was careful not to put him down for the count. The crowd was now yelling bloody murder. It was obvious that Dolf was able to toy with Ryan at will — at least so far.

In the second round, Champ apparently de-cided to try the newfangled boxing his trainers had tried to drill into him. He was dangerously fast for such a huge man. Late in the round, he caught Dolf high on the head with a lucky punch and staggered him so that his vision blurred and his speed left him for a moment while he tried to reorient his senses. Champ pressed his advantage with a series of pile-driver blows to the body. Dolf back-pedaled rapidly, covering himself, on the defensive for the first time. He was thankful to hear the bell. He was wondering if maybe he wouldn't have to take that dive. It would be no loss of stature to lose a fight to a real pro like Champ Ryan. Dolf resolved to carry the fight fair and square as many rounds as he could before taking that dive, if he had to.

There was a feeling in the crowd before the start of round three that this could turn out to be a real fight after all. Encouraged by his wildly cheering backers and a lucky midround knockdown of Dolf, he carried the fight to Dolf all the way.

Back in his corner, Knucks told Dolf, "Better get on that hoss. Tire the bastard out. Stay away from him. You've got plenty of time to put on a show yet. At least let *him* know you can take him."

"What makes you so sure I can? I been kicked by a mule and it felt better than his punches."

249

"You can take him all right. You just got overconfident, or careless. Get on that hoss and get the big blubber wobbly in his legs."

Taking Knucks's advice, by round eight Dolf had Ryan walking flat-footed, grimly plodding after him. The intervening rounds had been like round one; Dolf had been in command of the ring. When he returned to his corner at the end of that round, Dolf recognized that there had been some excitement going on there. Will was with Knucks when Dolf sat down on his stool. He yelled through the ropes, "We got Diana back. Clemmy just phoned." She'd stayed home in case a call came.

Dolf's heart took a huge leap inside him. He knew then what had been putting lead in his feet and arms. He waved a glove at Will and took a huge breath, exhaling explosively with relief.

"Okay, boy," Knucks said. "Go in and take him out." When the bell rang, Dolf glided to meet the Champ, feeling fresher than he had at round one. He hardly felt his feet touch the mat. He hammered away with a series of left jabs and right crosses, knowing the Champ would lose his temper as usual and charge him just as he had before. This time he had no intention of pulling the final punch, and if one haymaker didn't do it, he intended to unload on him like a summer cloudburst, with lefts and rights to the head once he'd softened him up. He didn't feel the least bit tired.

For that reason he was little short of amazed to "come to" in his dressing room, flat on his back, with a doctor working over him. He could dimly make out the wobbly figures of Will, Wyatt, and Knucks all standing next to the table he was stretched out on, looking concerned. He tried to make his jaws work and couldn't at first. He managed a painful grin and finally got out, "What did he hit me with?"

"*He* didn't," the doctor said. "You were shot. Lucky it just grazed you — and that you got a hard head. No concussion. I got the bleeding stopped and patched you up. You should have less trouble with it than you would have if Champ had landed one of those roundhouses he was swinging at you. Maybe less. I was out there watching. Lucky for you he didn't connect with one of those haymakers."

"Amen," Dolf agreed. He turned his head toward his friends. "Who the hell shot me? Did you get him?"

Before they could answer, the doctor continued, "I'll stay here awhile till you feel like getting up, then I want you to try walking around a little bit so I can tell for sure how you're doing."

Dolf was surprised to see Hanratty enter the room. The captain called, "Oh, Will. I wanta talk to you."

Will went over and was in earnest conversation with him for some time near the door.

Dolf said again, "Is anybody gonna tell me who shot me?"

"We don't know," Wyatt said. "We're still huntin', or that is, the cops are. Somebody cut the lights off just after the shot. The bastard had to have someone in cahoots with him; probably an inside job."

"Let me see if I can get on my pins," Dolf said while he was digesting that information. "Boy," he complained trying to get up, "my head feels like an elephant stepped on it."

The doctor came over hurriedly. "Maybe we'd better put you in the hospital. Can never tell in these cases. Just to be on the safe side."

Will was just returning from his confab with Hanratty and heard that. "Uh-uh," he objected. "Safer out at my place. Somebody may have another go at him. We can put you up in your old room on the third floor, Dolf." Dismissing that as decided, he turned to Wyatt and Knucks. "I'd appreciate your picking up Gabe and coming out to the house. I just got a real earful from Hanratty. Best we talk. I want you all to hear what Diana's got to say, too."

The doctor came along out to Will's to be sure that Dolf followed orders and went straight to bed. Before he left, he shook hands with Dolf. "That was a great fight," he said. "Maybe you'll have a rematch. My money'll be on you next time."

"Thanks," Dolf said. "Only there ain't gonna be a next time. I've got my bellyful of the ring — got sandbagged into that one against my will."

Will invited the whole group up to Dolf's room, where he was propped up with pillows behind him. Diana managed a few minutes with Dolf alone first. She regarded him with large, concerned eyes, stooping and kissing him gently.

"I'd die if you were killed," she said in a low voice next to his ear. She kissed him again.

He thought practically, she really wouldn't, but he was grateful for the sentiment. He could understand how she felt. He wondered, from his great sense of relief that she was safe, if perhaps he hadn't been cynical and self-serving with his doubts about her. At this moment he felt very much as he had the first night they were together. All he said was "You're no happier that I'm alive than I am that you are." Just then the others arrived.

Diana told her story first, including what they already knew from Victoria's prior account. "After Victoria left, I sat down and put Mr. Pookay's pistol in the drawer right next to me."

"Hold on," Dolf interrupted. "What's this about Pookay?"

"He's the one I got to rent me the place," Diana explained. "I heard about him because you told me you knew him. I've no idea why he came back there. Maybe to rob the place, and we walked in on him."

Dolf allowed her to continue, but he was rapidly turning over in his mind the significance of Pookay's being involved. Diana went on, "I'd no more than sat down when the door flew open and three Chinamen ran in. I tried to get the gun again, but they grabbed me too quick and finally tied and gagged me, although I put up the best fight I could."

"How'd they get you out with no one seeing you?" Dolf asked. "I checked at the other apartments — no one was home on the second floor, but the woman on the first hadn't seen or heard a thing."

Diana grinned. "There was somebody home on the second floor all right. That's where the Chinese took me and Mr. Pookay. They'd rented the place before then. I heard you knock and tried to make some noise but couldn't. They didn't take us out of there till after dark.

I've no idea what they did with Mr. Pookay, but they took me to a house in the hills behind Oakland. I'd probably still be there, but it belongs to Mammy Pleasant — our butler Eustace sometimes does jobs for her on his day off — so he just happened to come over and look at the place since it was vacant. I was in a closet and heard him moving around. I didn't know if it was some of the Chinese, but I kicked the door anyhow and made as much noise as I could. He got me out of there and untied me. We got away before the Chinese came back, if they were even planning to. Maybe they planned to just leave me. Anyhow, we went to the police, and they're out watching the place in case they do come back. The Oakland Police brought me home. That's about all there is to it."

"It's enough," Will said. "From what you told Hanratty earlier this evening, he figures Little Pete's crowd from Chinatown was at least mixed up in it, if they didn't plan the whole thing. Whether Pookay was in with them or not is hard to say. Now, if you ladies'll leave us alone awhile, I've got some plans to work out with Dolf and these three."

Dolf wondered how Will and his old enemy Hanratty had suddenly become so thick. He was unaware — as was Will, for that matter — that the police captain could feel the skids greased under his big flat feet. Hanratty suspected what Little Pete was up to with Buckley, and why. He'd also taken a terrible tongue-lashing from Buckley for having left town without his okay. The captain was looking for new political allies, ready to switch allegiance, particularly since he'd already decided he wasn't going to stay around much longer anyhow.

"I got an earful from Hanratty tonight after he talked to Diana and came down to the fight," Will said. "He's runnin' scared, if I'm any judge. Something's botherin' him awful bad. He told me who he's been takin' orders from higher up. It's Chris Buckley. I thought the bastard was my friend. But Hanratty doesn't know who's behind Buckley. I do. It's that old SOB Huntington. He even got wind of something and canceled his trip out here. Maybe he thinks we'd get him as an accessory to kidnapping. I would, too, if I could — and he knows it. You can bet he heard all about what's happened the past couple of days. My guess is it'll be a long time before old Collis P. graces us with his presence. In any case, I'm gonna knock that bastard Buckley off his perch. The Democratic party'll kick his ass out in a minute when they find out he's been toadying up to Huntington. And me 'n a few friends'll see enough money spread around to stiffen the party's backbone. But first I'm gonna deal with Little Pete for kidnapping Diana. I want you along, Dolf, so we'll wait till you're up on your pins."

Dolf nodded. "Probably tomorrow. I feel a lot better already."

"Don't rush it. Give it as long as you need. Hanratty told me something else that'll make you want to be in top shape when we go down there and bust in on that damn bastard. He's been hidin' out your old friend Twead in his own place. Hanratty's gonna find out for me if Twead is still there for sure. Pete'll try to wiggle out by blamin' the kidnapping on some other tong. Who else but Buckley and Little Pete, from what we know, would want Dolf out of town as part of the ransom? And the deal to throw the fight smells of Little Pete's tactics all the way. You and me know, Wyatt, he's always tryin' to fix the horse races, too. Throwing a fight is exactly his speed. We'll hit the little son of a bitch right in his own lair."

All of this gave Dolf plenty to think about before he went to sleep. He had another pressing concern. What to do about two women, both of whom he was immoderately fond of but wasn't sure he was in love with, in either case — or, if he was, which one. When he finally did get to sleep, he slept soundly.

# Chapter 19

If Dolf had been aware that his premonitions were correct and that Margaret and their son were indeed still alive back in Alaska, he'd have departed on the next boat, even if it meant letting Twead get away. And it certainly would have relieved his perplexity about Diana and Victoria. As it was, the possibility existed that he might marry one of them – with disastrous consequences for everyone, especially Margaret.

Margaret's attitude, stranded as she was in the Yukon wilderness, had alternated between lonely despondency and elation at the possibility that everything would eventually work out. She often imagined herself and little Henry reunited with Dolf. Fortunately, she had learned how to be patient, first during the long exile of her tribe in the Indian Nations, and then when she'd been sent to the white man's school for Indians at Carlisle, Pennsylvania. She had spent almost eight years there without seeing her family yet had been an avid student. Nonetheless, she had ultimately returned to *her people*. Something deep in her heart had impelled her to return, something more than simple love of family. She had heard people at the school say she was going back to the "blanket" and wasting herself. She hadn't cared. Once home, only the powerful pull of her love for Dolf had persuaded her to leave again.

Her people held the absolute belief that when you save someone's life, you belong to that person thereafter. Margaret had been as much responsible as anyone for keeping Dolf alive when he'd been brought to the camp of her father, Chief Henry, wounded and on the brink of death. In nursing him she had become his, with all the consuming intensity of the women of her race, accentuated by her own ardently devoted nature. Ever since, she had been ready to fight and die for him. She had proved this when she dived from a high cliff into the unplumbed, rocky depths of the Yukon rapids after Dolf and little Henry, who'd gone adrift in a scow. She had saved them from almost certain drowning in the awesome turbulence of Miles and Whitehorse Canyons. She had been expert at maneuvering a boat in white water; Dolf had not, as she'd known. She'd had no choice in her eyes but to risk her life to save them.

Still, she knew that in the first place it had only been a misunderstanding that had thrown Dolf into her arms. Of this she had become painfully aware from once surreptitiously reading a letter to Dolf from a woman Margaret considered to be all that she was not, and never could be — Victoria Wheat. She thought of that letter often. The memory always caused a familiar, wrenching pain in her heart. Worse yet, she was sure that Dolf by now considered both her and their son dead. Why shouldn't he? So he would be free to look for Victoria Wheat again. They might already be married, she sometimes thought, and tears would come to her eyes. As Dolf went to sleep at the Alexander house in San Francisco, Margaret was lying awake in the Yukon night, wondering where he was, and if he was thinking of her. It was always worst at night, knowing she should be off looking for him. "I should leave first thing tomorrow," she told herself. Yet there were compelling reasons why she had to stay where she was, at least for a while.

She had tried to get a message to Dolf or their friend Doc Hennessey, who had saved her life delivering Henry. Her letter, sent downriver with passing prospectors, had come back much later, soiled and dog-eared, with the cryptic note scrawled on it that both Dolf and Doc had left the Sky Pilot diggings for "outside."

Maybe he'll come back looking for us, she thought hopefully. But she dreaded the suspicion that he never would, that he would be relieved that he no longer had to bear the stigma of being a "squawman." So she was trapped, both by this deep uncertainty inside herself and by her loyalty to Mama Borealis, the Chilkat woman who had been her midwife until Doc Hennessey had arrived. She remembered vividly the intense, perspiring face and frightened eyes of Mama, frantically trying to save Margaret's life when she'd discovered that the unborn Henry was lodged crosswise and would probably die if left in that position, taking Margaret's life, too. Later, Mama's people had again saved her life, and this time Henry's as well. They had rescued them in a perilous footrace across the ice breaking up in the Yukon River. Mother and son had been sucked beneath the ice, then miraculously cast up on an ice floe downstream, drenched, freezing, and almost drowned. Margaret had lain near death for days with pneumonia, though Henry had survived in fine shape.

Now it was Margaret's turn to serve her faithful friend. Mama was going to have a baby. Margaret knew that Mama had contracted tuberculosis, and the disease was progressing rapidly. They were now all living with Mama's new husband at this tribe's summer salmon-fishing grounds. It was Margaret's aim to get Mama's stubborn husband, Nunek, to take Mama to the village of St. John early, before the tribe moved back there for the winter. There she could adequately care for her and perhaps save her life. At the very least, she could keep her alive till her child was born and then, if Mama died, care for the child as if it were her own. But Nunek hesitated to leave his people so soon, especially in a good salmon year.

So loyalty alone would have prevented Margaret's leaving Mama Borealis in her trouble. But the other matter, that of her heart, stayed her hand from even trying to write again to let Dolf know she and Henry were alive. One part of her — the white learning — argued, "It isn't fair!" But another, ancient inner voice whispered, "Let Wakan Tanka decide." Besides, she had already more than once seen how it would be for Dolf with an Indian wife in his world. She had seen him knock down one man for his slighting remarks about an "injun." She knew he'd do it again whenever he had to. But other white men with white wives weren't condemned to bear that kind of perpetual burden. Their wives helped them, rather than hindered.

If he were aiming to live the contented sort of existence his friend Old John Hedley had in the backwater of St. John, with Elsie, the Sioux woman he'd brought to Alaska with him, it might be different. Squawmen were common in Alaska. A large part of Margaret's tragedy was that she simply could not believe Dolf when he had told her that this was exactly what he planned to do. He'd eagerly embraced the prospect, and hoped and planned for it until Margaret and Henry had disappeared without a trace. The thought that he'd lost all that had almost killed him. Further, Margaret couldn't always believe that Dolf would return with all possible haste even if he knew his family was alive, regardless of any other considerations.

So, in her desperate uncertainty, a voice urged her, "Return to your people next year. Go home *where you belong* and think your problem out." She was relieved that she wouldn't have to decide anything till fall. Having reached this conclusion, she slept fitfully, waking intermittently, her eyes wet with tears. She kept telling herself over and over, "I owe it to Dolf to free him."

Another problem, once she returned to St. John, would be how to persuade Elsie and Old John not to send Dolf the news that his family had miraculously escaped drowning. If she reached St. John late enough, the weather would temporarily solve the problem for her. No message could be sent out then till spring.

Despite her perplexity, deep inside she felt that Dolf truly loved her; admitted that if he knew they were alive he'd return at once.

"What's the matter with me then?" she heard her tortured voice almost scream inside of her. But only questions came back as her reply. Why hadn't he stayed to search — at least for one season? She didn't know that he had desperately combed the country for weeks before leaving on an urgent mission. Meanwhile she was finding it more and more possible to avoid the obvious answer to why he didn't come now — that he thought they were dead. Yet, she was trying desperately to convince herself that he simply didn't love her, because she knew that was the only way she would ever be able to free him. She was obsessed with the idea that she owed that to him. Sometimes she even rationalized herself into believing that he had never loved her. After all, he had come to her on the rebound. At those times, she seriously thought of killing both herself and Henry.

What kind of life would Henry have as a half-breed? she asked herself. Even worse than I have as a full-blood, she thought. As uncertain of things as she already was, if she had known Dolf's situation, caught between two beautiful women willing to marry him — one of them Victoria Wheat — she might have taken at least her own life. But she would not have done so until Mama's baby had come and until she could take the children back and place them in Elsie Hedley's care.

# Chapter 20

Dolf felt fine after a long sleep. Both Diana and Victoria came close to killing him with kindness when he insisted on getting up for breakfast. Clemmy watched all this with amused interest. She'd become very fond of Victoria.

"Are you sure you should be out of bed?" they'd all three asked Dolf.

"I feel great. I'm not sure I shouldn't be down running a few miles." Actually, he felt like a train had run over him — not from the gunshot wound, but rather from the battering the Champ had given his abdomen. But he didn't want to show it. He was anxious to go after Twead and didn't want Will to put off the showdown.

Will, who'd come home to see how Dolf was, joined them for a late breakfast. "Good," he'd responded to Dolf's appraisal of himself. "We'll make our hit tonight."

He assembled his small force at the Latin Quarter after dark. All but Will were surprised when Hanratty joined them as they were about to leave. Dolf reserved judgment on the wisdom of this move. He was certain that the captain had tried to have him shanghaied, but in Will's interest he'd let that pass.

"Official cloak," Hanratty stated. "I'll get you inside. The rest is up to you." He was thinking, but didn't add, And may the best man win.

His Annie should be about at Salt Lake City by then, he figured, headed for Boston on the train. The captain had decided to pull up stakes no matter what the outcome. Forty years had feathered his nest so he'd never have financial worries. By morning he'd be across the bay headed east in a palace car.

Little Pete's apartment occupied the second floor of a building taking up a quarter of a block. Hanratty rapped on the stairwell door and was greeted by a steel panel opening and a suspicious pair of Asian eyes looking him over. His companions were well out of sight in the shadows to one side.

"Ah so, Captain Hanratty," the voice greeted. The door opened. Hanratty rapped the Chinaman sharply over the head with a blackjack.

"C'mon in," he called. They followed Hanratty upstairs, where a second door confronted them, closed. Hanratty pushed an unobtrusive lever and the door swung inward. The room beyond was dimly lit and redolent of incense. A more brightly lit room down a hallway emitted the sound of voices.

They slipped down that direction on tiptoe and were surprised by a Boo How Doy who, thinking he heard something, stepped into the hall. Gabriel Dufan snatched him into the air in a stranglehold. He didn't utter a sound.

"Anybody out there?" Little Pete called after him without much conern in his voice. Getting no answer, he turned his eyes to the door. They opened wide with surprise and fear at the sight they beheld. He must have tripped a signal with his foot, since there was a sudden sound of running feet and excited voices from farther down the hall.

Hanratty stepped quickly to Little Pete and pushed a cocked pistol against the back of his head. "Sit still," he hissed. "Call your marines in here."

A Chinaman dressed like an American, pistol in hand, burst through the door before Little Pete could utter a squeak. The bodyguard's jaw dropped in stunned surprise. A second followed him, unable to arrest his momentum. The third let out a yelp and scurried back out of the light. Many pistols had covered them.

"Tell 'em to drop 'em and join the party," Hanratty ordered. This the tong leader quickly did.

"Call that other bastard back, too," Hanratty added.

When the last bodyguard was safely inside again and Gabriel had deposited their half-strangled partner in a chair, Hanratty nodded to Will. "It's your party from here on out."

"Any more of your sneaky sons of bitches staked out around here?" Will asked.

Little Pete shook his head. He was beginning to regain a degree of composure. When he'd first seen Hanratty, he'd figured it was going to be a rub-out of the variety the captain had become known for over the years. He'd assumed Hanratty had learned of his attempted double-cross with Buckley. Now, however, he began to hope he was going to live through this deal after all.

Will took over as invited. "Gabe, you and Knucks stay out in the hall just in case. I wouldn't trust this son of a bitch any farther than I could dropkick an anvil. Now — Pete, you little bastard, you had my daughter kidnapped. That ain't habit-forming. I might spare your scrawny neck if you produce that murdering little son of a bitch Twead."

Pete's eyes shifted uncomfortably, considering that. "He ain't here," he lied. "And I didn't kidnap your daughter, it was the Suey Sings."

"It figures you'd say that. Knucks, come in here a minute. Show this little bastard that operation on the neck you were showing us the other day."

Knucks pressed his thumbs into Little Pete's neck in just the right place and the Chinaman's eyes turned up into his head, his arms and legs flopping like those of a decapitated chicken.

"What'd ya do, Knucks, if I asked you to permanently paralyze the little piss ant?"

"Why, I'd do it, Will." He relaxed the grip long enough for Pete to hear that, then reapplied it, finally turning him loose. It took the Chinaman a half minute to reorient his senses.

"Do we get Twead?"

"Okay! He's down the hall, unless he heard the racket and cut out."

Twead had heard the racket but assumed it was some of the usual Chinese gabbing about gambling or women. The Boo How Doy were always threatening one another in shrill voices when Little Pete was out. Twead merely assumed he was out. So when his door opened, he thought at first it was some member of the establishment. He couldn't believe he was seeing Dolf Morgette. He started to reach for the pistol under his pillow, since he'd been reading, sprawled on the bed, then froze at the thought that he had almost committed suicide.

"C'mon along, Twead," Dolf said calmly, not even showing a gun. "I figured I'd blow a hole in you on sight, but I've been in the pen myself. Twenty years or so oughta be worse 'n dyin' for a high-flyer like you. You're goin' back to Montana."

When they got back to the others, Dolf booted him ahead of him into the room. He almost fell into Gabe's arms.

"Py Gar!" Gabe roared. He gave Twead a dose of the stranglehold the Boo How Doy had gotten a few minutes before.

"Now," Will said, "the party's almost over. I got one more thing to say to you." He speared Little Pete with a blunt forefinger. "If I ever have to come back here, I'm going to kill you so dead you'll stink before you hit the floor."

Little Pete's eyes were fixed on him with intense fear showing in them, but also relief to be getting off this easy. Nonetheless, in the back of his mind his hatred for Hanratty's setting him up was seething, unbalancing his normally calculating mind. He knew that if this crew left him sitting here, he could run down to the street door through a secret passage. His blood boiled to sink a hatchet in the Irishman's head even if it cost him his life. And it might not. With luck, if he moved quickly, he could strike, slam shut the front door, and disappear into the many subterranean passages beneath this whole area. He could flee to China and live the rest of his life in peace and luxury with Heavenly Flower.

His plan was foiled by Will's caution. "You won't mind seein' us out," he suggested. "We'll just keep a six-shooter behind yer ear in case you had any surprise plans for us."

The sapped doorman was just coming to as they reached the exit. Hanratty peered down at him as they filed out. "A good job if I do say it myself," he observed. This gave Little Pete his last chance. He pulled a dagger and raised it over Hanratty's back. Will, who still had his cocked pistol in hand, raised it swiftly and snapped off a shot. It almost missed Pete but luckily hit the hand with the knife. Pete dropped it, cursing. Hanratty spun around, jerking a pistol from under his coattail. He took in the scene instantly. Taking his time, he aimed the pistol between Little Pete's eyes and very slowly and deliberately eared back the hammer.

"No! No! Please!" Pete squealed.

"Bang!" Hanratty said, and laughed. He lowered the hammer again and buffaloed Little

Pete with the barrel alongside the ear. He stepped out and closed the door.

"I owe you one for that, Will," he said, re-pocketing his pistol. He held out his hand. As much for Will's sake as anyone's, he said, "I shudda killed the little bastard. But, hell, I don't even shoot dogs anymore. Musta killed a thousand in my day. Now I figger when I see a scrawney mongrel that maybe it's got a bunch o' pups somewhere that'll starve if I pull the trigger." This remark was his way of saying to Will, "Truce."

# EPILOGUE

As the Yukon steamer *Ira Baker* maneuvered into shore at St. John, Dolf was reviewing in his mind his farewell to San Francisco. His last parting with Diana had been very much like the first night together. Of course, there'd been the final bon voyage party for the whole family later.

"If you don't find Margaret," Diana had told him, "I'll be waiting. If you do, I'll be happy for you — and sad for me." She'd smiled wistfully. "I suppose I'll live, but it doesn't feel like it now." She'd laid her head on his bare shoulder and he could feel her warm tears trickling on him. But she wasn't the type to feel sorry for herself for long. She'd recovered quickly and drew him on top of her.

Victoria had been a vastly different proposition. She fully understood how it would probably have to be. He wasn't really sure how she was taking that inside. He was sure she was all woman and wanted him again before they parted, perhaps forever. She had openly come to his apartment and stayed a lot longer than she could the first time. Her last words to him had been "Whatever happens, I'll always love you, Dolf. There may have to be someone else — that's the way life is — but every woman holds someone special in her heart. If they're lucky, it's the one they marry. If they aren't, and most aren't, there's always that golden memory. You're that one, Dolf."

He hadn't known what to say. There was little to say that would help. Finally he said, "It might have been that way for us. Maybe it still will."

She hadn't cried. She'd kissed him gently, then fiercely, and walked away, her back straight, and never turned back once. He didn't know that she hadn't turned to wave because tears blinded her eyes and she didn't want him to pity her.

He'd made a lot of friends in San Francisco, even Champ Ryan, Hanratty, and Mornet. The captain told Dolf what Little Pete had confided to him of Twead's two other attempts to get him with a rifle, at the Palace and by the Cliff House. He also sweated Twead for the information that it had been he who had potshot Dolf from ringside.

Hanratty had suggested, "We can send him up right here if you want." But Dolf wanted the Parrents back in Montana to have the satisfaction of seeing Twead punished back where he'd had Harvey murdered. Maybe they'll swing him, Dolf thought. In a way, that'd be best.

As for Pookay, he'd disappeared, maybe into the bay permanently. The only mystery remaining was who had doused the lights after Twead had potshot him at the Union Exchange. Twead simply wouldn't tell.

Two special friends had been Knucks and Gabe. Dolf hadn't had to say an unhappy goodbye to them. They were on board the *Ira Baker* with him.

Like Dolf, Wyatt Earp wasn't much for talk. Their farewell had been a drink and a handshake. "I expect I'll see yuh around someday, Dolf," Wyatt had said. "Good luck."

Last of all had been Will and Clemmy — perhaps, in a way, harder to part with than Diana and Victoria. As usual he hadn't known what to say. Clemmy had kissed him, then held his shoulders between her hands, looking at him tearfully. "We love you, Dolf. All of us. Come home again," she'd said. He nodded silently. Will simply shook hands and growled, "Come back, Dolf — if you can. We'll miss the hell outa yuh."

Nonetheless, when he docked at St. John, he felt he was really coming home. Something in the awesome, silent vastness of Alaska called him back, even despite the tragedy of having lost his family there. The great silver sheet of water wound upstream toward the deep green hills, dressed here and there with brilliant streaks of aspens, the river itself bordered by yellow and red willows. All whispered, "Welcome back." He took a huge breath of the invigorating cold air, tangy with the smell of autumn. "Home," he told himself. "Even without Maggie and the kid" — he'd heard not a word of them anywhere on the way in. He at least looked forward to seeing John and Elsie Hedley and Dan Quillen and his big, rangy son, Ave.

Margaret Morgette had occupied Doc Hennessey's empty cabin with Mama Borealis and her man since mid-August. Margaret had persuaded him to bring her to St. John ahead of the tribe's move because of her advancing tuberculosis and her pregnancy. There Mama had had her girl on September first, lived only three weeks, and died quietly in her sleep, the baby still sleeping contentedly in her cold, stiff arms when morning came. Her last words to Margaret the night before had been "I think I git betta. Be all well tomarra. I lub you."

They had buried her high on the crest of the hill behind the cabin, overlooking miles of the Sky Pilot and Yukon Valleys and range after range of rolling forested hills. Margaret had found a wet nurse for Mama's daughter, whom her mother had insisted they name after Margaret. It was understood with Nunek, Mama's husband, that in the event of her death the baby was to be raised by Margaret. He had stoically accepted his loss and departed to join the village of his people and find another wife, which he probably would do before winter.

Margaret's heart had received a vast lift from the depths of her depression the day following Mama's death. A San Francisco *Chronicle* had arrived on an upriver steamer. In it she read: DOLF MORGETTE WILL FIGHT CHAMP RYAN. *One of the first bouts anywhere under the new fifteen three-minute round rules. Wyatt Earp will referee.* The article went on to say that Dolf had come to town from Alaska and was rumored to be on the trail of a fugitive. It gave her heart the mighty lift it needed. She felt like singing. She continued to read, *Morgette is in the employ of the well-known Will Alexander, at whose Union*

*Exchange the bout will be held.* But the closing remark in the article delivered a death blow to her short-lived elation. It read: *It is reliably heard that Morgette, who lost his wife in Alaska last spring, will marry Will Alexander's daughter, Diana. He is considered a very lucky man by everyone. Miss Alexander is one of the reigning beauties of the coast and due, someday, to inherit her family's fortune.*

If it hadn't been for her responsibility to her son, Henry, and young Margaret, she'd have killed herself gladly. This piece of news convinced her, as nothing else had, that Dolf had been her whole life, despite her frequent wavering resolves to leave him for his own good. But now she knew that she must do that at last. She remembered her father's message: "Come home to your people."

*"I'll go home to my people,"* she told herself. "Home for good."

She was packing to make the outbound trip on the *Ira Baker* when Dolf arrived. The steamer would go upriver one day and she'd catch it on the way back. Elsie Hedley told Dolf where he'd find Margaret. He'd almost swooned to hear the news that she was alive.

"How?" he'd almost shouted.

"Let her tell you," Elsie said. "She's over in Skookum Doc's cabin."

He didn't knock. She had her back turned, changing little Margaret's diaper on the bed. She was annoyed to be disturbed; all she wanted was to be left alone after reading about Dolf.

He approached and stood close behind her, saying nothing. She turned and found him grinning his old grin at her.

"Dolf!" she cried. She wasn't sure it wasn't a ghost.

Young Henry looked on, not quite sure he shouldn't run for help. Then the stranger grabbed him up in his arms and hugged him and his mother, who, for some reason, had started to cry.

Young Henry yelled at the top of his lungs, pushing Dolf away and trying to pummel him.

Dolf laughed. "He's a Morgette all right. I got the right cabin for sure."